Failing Gravity

Books by Jordan S. Keller

Failing Gravity

Ashes Over Avalon Trilogy
Wildfire
Burnout
Combustion

For more information
visit: www.SpeakingVolumes.us

Failing Gravity

Jordan S. Keller

SPEAKING VOLUMES, LLC
NAPLES, FLORIDA
2025

Failing Gravity

Copyright © 2025 by Jordan S. Keller

All rights reserved. No part of this book may be reproduced or transmitted in any form or by any means without written permission.

ISBN 979-8-89022-297-8

For my mom, Maja,
who's won every battle with kindness

Chapter One

Roman Koa didn't appreciate being owed money.

Discarded plastics crunched under his boots as he crossed the cracked and corroded street. Neon lights flickered against the remnants of the old-world city and littered the ground in smears of blue, green, and red light. More neon tubing crisscrossed around him, reflecting off every metallic surface of the Slums. The glow had once been beautiful to him, but Roman knew what it really was: a disguise. Something to mask the junkyard of a city. He didn't mind. Roman had stopped minding things years ago.

He stopped pretending the Slums was anything but a trash-infested playground, too.

Roman jogged up the front steps of an apartment. All the dwellings on this side of town were made from brick, and iron fencing wrapped around the ground level to protect the first-floor windows. They were nice for the Slums. Some apartments even had a light burning above the door to ward off criminals and pests. Roman rolled his eyes at the superstitious warning. Cotton candy-scented tobacco smoke oozed out from under the door. Light didn't shine from any of the cracks around the frame or through the curtained windows, but the smoke confirmed Evanston was home. Roman didn't knock—pleasantries were the first thing to go in these situations—and kicked in the door. Someone inside shrieked and several half-naked bodies scurried off the sofa in the center of the room. They moved like cockroaches, diving into shadows and leaving their prized pizza crust for a predator to claim.

A lone candle on the floor illuminated the remaining man who choked on the inhale of his hookah. Evanston's cheeks burned red, and his eyes swelled. The tiny pupils shook inside their watery hold. Roman grinned. Fear of choking wasn't what overtook the bookie. That accomplishment belonged to Roman Koa.

"Roman!" Evanston greeted after composing himself. "What can I do for you?"

"Cut it." Roman crossed the room and loomed over Evanston. The bookie sunk deeper into the sofa, adding useless distance between them. "Where's my scratch?"

"I already gave it to Scrap." Evanston's lie was as evident as the burns on his fingertips. "The day I owed it, I sent it over to your guy, like always. He must have taken it!"

Roman kicked the tall hookah sitting between them. Hot coals and sharp glass scattered across the floor, and he yanked the hose from Evanston's boney fingers. "You're a liar and a thief. You know I don't like either."

Evanston flinched at the shattered glass but kept lying. "The credits must not have sent properly. The service down here sucks, you know that. Icaria transmissions always getting in the way. Let me send them again."

"Don't forget the extra twenty percent."

Roman took joy in the way Evanston's eyes widened. "Twenty percent? That's more than my commission! Hell, that's higher than any bookie here!"

"Consider it a service charge for me having to make a home visit." Roman leaned in closer, catching every stench that clung to Evanston. The sweet-scented smoke did little to hide what he really was. A parasite. "Unless you want me to take this place off your hands instead."

Evanston's Adam's apple bulged as he swallowed. "Right, of course. Let me grab my Pada."

Roman didn't move as Evanston got off the couch, forcing the man to slide over the back and crumble to the floor. Once across the room,

Evanston grabbed something off the counter: a digital screen about the size of his hand. Roman crossed his arms, tapping his tattooed fingers against himself as Evanston fumbled with his Pada. Only the out-of-date models were sold in the Slums, and the high-pitched whine of the processor signaled it'd be a few minutes. Using the technology inside any of the Slums' watering holes ensured a quicker connection to the server if a home didn't have antennas. Roman looked around the room, at the filth that grew from every inch, and wondered why a man like Evanston hadn't upgraded. The bookie had fat and deep pockets from working with the fighters. Most of the other bookies lived in a gated neighborhood closer to the center of the Slums. Closer to Icaria.

A glowing coal caught Roman's attention, and he remembered the guest scurrying away when he arrived. The bookie's pockets weren't deep enough for his habits, it seemed. Roman nudged the coal away from a pile of wrinkled newspapers. He didn't care if Evanston burned, but the other people here hadn't earned Roman's rage. They were just trying to survive like he was.

"That new Icaria fighter is debuting tonight," Evanston said, chancing a glance at Roman over the hazy light emitted from the Pada's screen. "I could put all this scratch on you to win and we'd both be rich. I know the bets are leaning in his favor."

A grumble boiled at the back of Roman's throat. He wasn't sure if the annoyance was coming from Evanston's stalling or at the mention of another sunkisser trying to claim his spot in the ring. Probably both. "I won't ask for my scratch a second time."

Evanston tapped on his Pada for another minute. "There. Debt's paid."

Roman flicked his wrist to check the Pada he wore duct-taped to his arm. Most slummers kept their Padas in a pocket or hanging off a chain around their necks, but he preferred the security the tape provided. If anyone tried taking the thin digital screen, he'd know. And the would-be thief would be in easy striking distance. Roman's account showed the newest increase of cryptens. He could have left it there, the money was paid, but Roman had a few minutes left to kill before he needed to leave for tonight's fight. He lowered his arm and approached Evanston. His long gait got him there in three easy steps. Roman snatched Evanston's hand and pulled two fingers violently back.

"Hey! Hey!" Evanston shouted as the backs of his fingers pointed toward his arm. "Roman, stop!"

Roman didn't. Evanston's fingers popped then slammed against the back of his hand. The bookie yowled like an injured cat. Roman released him and shoved him into the wall, wiping his hands down the front of his shirt in case any of Evanston clung to him.

Roman pinned the bookie with a satisfactory look. He would remember this day; even when they healed, the broken fingers would make sure of it. Every bookie who wanted to steal from Roman would remember, too. He shouldn't have used their services, but at first it was hard for an oil-stained slummer like him to negotiate bets with the sunkissers alone. That was before he had started winning, before anyone noticed him. Before the slummers started calling him King and the Icarians learned to fear his next robot. He didn't need a bookie anymore. Roman left the apartment.

The Slums enveloped Roman. Each street looked like the one before it. All of them hiding under Icaria's floating disk which shrouded the city in shadows, filth, and a lack of developments. Buildings constructed lifetimes ago were patched with sheet metal, brick, forgotten old-world materials, and whatever Icaria discarded into the landfills. Windows were backlit by more neon. People moved past each other with one hand gripping a weapon while the other protected their belongings. Only the most desperate stole from other slummers, but all times were desperate here.

Some days, the streets were wide and picked over. Other days they were narrow and filled with new trash dumped by Icaria, ready to be salvaged or scavenged. Roman grew up digging through every trash heap looking for something to do, something to sell, something to eat, anything to elevate him. Most of those early days he was left empty-handed.

Now Roman knew which heaps to really dig into. Which piles of filth would reward him with new parts, new material, new ammunition. He hadn't been to the main dump in years. He knew climbing through that muck would only supply him with rotten food and probably the need for an antibiotic shot. The main trash chute of Icaria was for the most desperate, too. He knew which chutes were worth his time.

His Pada vibrated against his forearm alerting Roman to new messages. He glanced at the display screen while jumping over a small fissure in the street. None of the unread messages were friendly. Each one was a slummer offering Roman a job. Most paid well, and a younger Roman would have accepted them immediately, but his upcoming fight was more important. Whatever they needed could wait until Roman floated down from the high he would be experiencing after he won.

The neon lights strapped to the underside of Icaria paled ghostly white as he neared the Ring. The old-world sporting arena was repurposed for a new-aged blood bath. A thick electrical wire connected the top of the Ring's domed roof to the bottom of Icaria, several hundred feet above. The energy inside the wire hummed loud enough to keep the rats away and caused the wire to glow a bright white. The Ring was one of the few places in the Slums kept clean and well lit. Roman knew it wasn't out of any sense of pride. The types of barbaric activities that took place inside were outlawed in Icaria. It didn't mean the sunkissers living in luxury above the Slums had no desire to watch or participate in the fights. Icaria sanitationists came down once a month to clean the area. Roman pilfered their trucks enough times to learn the schedule.

Several Icarian carriages were parked outside the Ring's circular drive. The white chrome exteriors were already slick with grime and grease. Roman wondered if, after they were done here, they bothered cleaning the carriages or just tossed them out to not get their hands dirty. Standing beside one, Roman drew a four-pointed crown in the grime. If the carriage did fall back to the Slums, his tag would become his claim on it. An uppercase B had been carved into the wheel hub of a carriage next to him.

Roman straightened his back. If Bruno was here, then there were more than robot fighters to watch out for. The dust runner could be refilling his taps or lurking in the shadows. Either option was bad news for the sunkissers. Roman grinned.

The usual crowd of people lingered outside the Ring's front entrance and parted for Roman as he approached. A few shouted "good luck" and a few more shouted that he didn't need any. Several held crumpled tickets in their fists. Several more looked between the door and the ticket taker gauging the speed needed to get past both undetected. The bright lights kept shadows from leaking into the building, but Roman waltzed through the front door anyway.

The hallway was well lit, and it made Roman squint. On any other fight night, half the lights would be off to save power, but tonight everything was on full display for the sunkissers and their champion. Probably some CEO, or royal daughter, or an inventor of another groundbreaking device the slummers would never own. Every other month it happened; some new sunkisser fighter would register for a week on the bracket, secure the nicest prep room, and be gone after the first fight with their tail between their legs. No one lasted more than a match against Roman.

The hall deposited him into a long room full of booths selling food, trinkets, and recovered items found in junk piles. Digital screens hung high on the walls behind iron cages and played a video of the Icarian president reminding everyone of the proper rules of Icarian society, but no one came here for order. As a boy, Roman thought President Hinge watched him through the screens until he realized the video feed was on a loop. Several of the screens had been graffitied to black Hinge's eyes or teeth. Only two were done by Roman who had given the man deep slanted eyebrows and fangs to make sure everyone knew how corrupt he really was.

The earthy smell of grilling mushrooms tickled Roman's nose, but he turned away from the food stall. Eating before a fight always made him queasy. He passed a booth selling broken robot parts as souvenirs and spotted the yellow casing of a bot he'd destroyed a week ago. The damage had been so severe that night he hadn't realized anything was left.

It wasn't too long ago that bits of his own bots were sold in places like this. Laid out in a reminder of his defeat. The clerk offered him a tight smile before rearranging the merchandise to entice a sale.

Beside that booth, two sunkissers were being overcharged for a piece of trash they probably threw out themselves. Roman laughed.

The man, overdressed in silks, tapped his sleek Pada against the clerk's cracked, out-of-date version and both devices chirped after the cryptens successfully transferred. The clerk wrapped their purchases in an old piece of paper and handed it to the waiting woman, who tucked it inside her purse. Having an authentic piece of the Slums would wow their friends back home. It'd make them cultured. They probably felt good about helping a slummer with their business. Their true colors shone a bit differently under these lights; it wasn't about helping anyone other than themselves.

The couple turned from the booth, and Roman went out of his way to walk into one of them. They could get their kicks in the Slums all they wanted, but he wouldn't let them forget what this place truly was. A jungle. A place where he was king. The man's mouth hung open, any response forgotten as he took in Roman's appearance.

Red leather strips laced his boots, black pants tucked in at the top. A black tank showed off various tattoos printed on his arms and neck. One of the tattoos was a green serpent wrapping around his right forearm until the head opened atop his hand and spread its two fangs across his thumb and pointer finger. His left eyebrow sported a fresh split from an earlier incident and his solemn expression dared the man to speak.

"Excuse you," the woman said first, her nose twisted up in the expression Roman was used to seeing on a sunkisser trying to look down at him despite his height.

Roman crossed his arms, making his frame take up more of the walkway.

"Do you mind?" The woman wasn't asking to be polite. "Do you know who we are?"

"No." And Roman didn't care to find out.

"Pardon us," the man finally squeaked, leading his companion away. As they retreated, Roman heard the pair hissing in whispers. The woman looked over her shoulder at Roman before the man pulled her down the hallway. "That's him. That's the robot killer. Don't make a scene."

Roman chuckled. After they rounded a corner, he removed the watch he'd yanked from inside the man's jacket and lifted it to his ear. Tiny gears ticked away the seconds, and the small solar panel on the back promised a reliable battery anywhere else than the Slums, which hadn't seen actual sunlight since Icaria was constructed above them a century ago. Roman slid the watch into his back pocket. The solar panel would probably be useless, but the smaller springs and gears could be useful.

Leaving the trinket booths and food stalls, Roman made his way to the lower level of the Ring to the fighter's rooms. Each competitor from the Slums rented a bathroom-sized space for final preparations before the steel doors opened to the fighting arena in the center of the dome. The sport was a free-for-all battle where only one victor remained. Most went home empty-handed, their fighters too wrecked to salvage any parts. Roman approached the door marked with his four-pointed crown. He hovered his Pada over the lock until it opened.

"Watch out!"

Roman ducked and nearly avoided a saw blade flying through the air that would've taken off his head. The blade slammed into the wall behind him, sticking out several inches and becoming an eyesore on the otherwise spotless walkway. Roman slammed the door.

"Sorry about that, Ro," apologized the other boy in the room.

The mechanic's hands were wrist-deep inside a machine leaking oil onto a table. More oil splattered against his T-shirt as he tried to stop the flow. The rag slung over his shoulder dripped more of it down his back and onto the floor.

"That better not be mine," Roman said.

The mechanic pointed over his shoulder. His robotic fingers squealed with the extra lubrication of the oil. The silver appendages met flesh about halfway up his forearm. "Sphere would never leak this much."

Roman ran his hand over the spherical device the mechanic had pointed at. It was about the size of a basketball and looked incredibly unassuming. The silver-and-black patch worked outer shell was as scratch free as the first day Roman debuted the bot. That was the same day he won over five thousand cryptens and started his reign as champion.

"Ran specs when I first got here," the mechanic continued, refusing to look away from his hemorrhaging project. "Fully charged and ready to go."

"Good." Roman lowered his hand. "What about that thing?"

The mechanic yanked a tube from inside the motor. The spilling oil morphed from a geyser to a drip. "I'm not ready to give up on her yet."

Roman tossed a cleaner towel at him. "If anyone will figure it out, it's you, Scrap."

"Thanks man, but flattery will only get you a cheap night with one of Cee's girls. Not me." Scrap wiped his hands clean, taking extra time around each of his bolted knuckles. "Did'ya see Evanston?"

Roman grinned. "Yeah. I got what I deserved and so did he."

"I would've come with you." Scrap set the towel down. "One day, one of the bookies might have a bodyguard bigger and scarier than you."

Roman laughed. Any extra scratch Evanston had that he could have spent on protection would've gone to one of his habits. The only people bigger and scarier than Roman wouldn't be working for a bookie anyway. Roman watched Scrap continue to clean oil from himself, the table, his malfunctioning motor. He didn't want anyone on his jobs anyway. People got in the way.

"Since you're out of commission tonight, run bets for me." It wasn't a request.

"I'll bleed them sunkissers dry." Scrap grinned. Somehow, even his teeth hadn't avoided the oil spill. After a gesture from Roman, he ran the rag against his gums. "They're throwing all kinds of scratch around for this new fighter to win."

"They're that sure of this guy?" Part of Roman thought Evanston had lied to him about the heavy weight of the bets. If Scrap was confirming it, then this new fighter must be packing something decent. Maybe tonight would be interesting.

Scrap nodded. "Yeah, so says Canon's man. Says he came down here to beat you specifically. Says all of Icaria knows about you."

Roman smirked, feeling ten feet taller. Good. He wanted the sunkissers to know about what he'd done. Without them. All on his own inside a junkyard.

"I heard two of them talking about how tonight will be your last night. Apparently, the guy's got the best bot cryptens can buy."

Roman cocked an eyebrow. "What do you think?"

"I think the guy is gonna wish he spent his scratch on something else. People can't buy what you've created, Ro. Hey," Scrap flexed his metal prosthetic, "maybe tonight I get thirty percent of the cut?"

Roman leveled his gaze on Scrap. The younger boy's smile wavered slightly but he didn't break eye contact. Above them, the intercom buzzed a ten-minute warning.

"Twenty is still good for me, Ro." Scrap retracted his statement. "With all the scratch you're about to win, it'll feel like a bonus anyway."

Roman nodded in agreement and sat in front of his sphere. "Go make our bets."

"Roger that." Scrap tried wiping his hands clean again before tossing the rag over his robot. "I'll find you after the fight."

After Scrap left, Roman ran his own diagnostics on his robot. Scrap was a decent slummer. He never tried to pull anything over on him, but Roman wasn't in the business to turn soft. He'd seen more than one robot sabotaged before a fight. After his readings came back clear, he kicked his feet up and waited. The other slum bots would be ammo fodder for his sphere, but the Icaria bots could be a problem. The floating city kept better weapons for themselves, just like they kept better food, medicine, education, and clean water.

He couldn't wait to slaughter their bots and their too-righteous attitude with a robot made from their trash. Roman would remain king of the Ring.

Chapter Two

After the ten minutes were up, Roman's prep room door swung open to the arena. The overhead lights flooded the room and burned his eyes when he stepped out, joining the other slummers on the ground level. His sunkisser opponents would descend from their top-floor prep rooms mirroring their arrival into the Slums.

The uproar of the crowd deafened Roman. It amazed him he hadn't heard the noise inside his prep room, but now he reveled in it. There was a full house. The bets would be high. It would be easy money. The crowd was still hungry even after four opening fights. He shifted his sphere onto his hip and stepped onto his riser.

The riser floated him to a steel platform suspended halfway between the floor and ceiling. The platform balanced atop four anti-gravity stations at the corners, bathing the floor and underside in hazy blue light, using the same technology that levitated Icaria. Roman could barely hear the hum of energy under the excited crowd in the stands positioned around the arena. Plenty of people cheered his name, plenty more cheered his title. He pulled his shoulders farther back and held his chin high.

They wanted a king, so he would be their king.

A hexagonal chain-link fence ran along the sides of the platform before tapering off at the ceiling. Initially, the fence was the only protection between the fight and the crowd. After a bolt slipped through the fence and embedded in someone's eyes, a force field was put up to protect the more expensive ticket holders. It was a gift from Icaria.

When Roman was a boy and a stray piece of metal sliced his arm open, no one bothered increasing the barrier. Some sunkisser told him to not bleed on his shoes when the fight ended and everyone left. The scar healed into an off-white smear while the memory fueled his hatred.

The other fighters levitated to their positions around the arena and stepped off their risers. Only a thin metal platform kept the fighters from falling. Roman lazily eyed his opponents. It was easy to tell who belonged and who didn't. Who was from the Slums and who descended from Icaria for a night of wanton endangerment. Who knew how to pilot a bot and who had purchased one on a whim.

Standing on Roman's right was one of the latter. The woman's dress looked more expensive than the bird-shaped robot tucked under her arm, both the same shade of turquoise. She waved at the crowd and received a couple of hollers from men and women wearing the same shade of blue. Roman rolled his eyes. His livelihood was some fun Friday night out for them. No matter how stupid the bird bot looked, it probably cost enough cryptens to feed him for a year.

A display board hung from the ceiling and ranked the night's competitors. Roman's name was at the top next to a photo that matched the headshot on his lost entry badge. His expression was dangerous, his grin was sharp, his eyes were set to kill.

His four-pointed crown was spray-painted on the floor of the arena. The sunkissers could buy whatever upgrades to the Ring they wanted, but they would never own it like he did.

He broke in every night to repaint his crown until they stopped painting over it.

"Ladies and gentlemen!" An announcer's voice rang out from the overhead speakers. "Welcome to Fight Night, the only place left in the world to witness such carnage, such devastation, such havoc as a robot battle. There're still a few minutes to place your bets on tonight's fighters. We've got several returning faces tonight, including our own King of the Ring, Roman Koa!"

The slummers standing on the lowest level who couldn't afford actual seats raised their fists and bellowed their support. They packed the floor like ants on a rotten fruit rind. One of the sunkissers across the arena from Roman rolled his eyes at the response. A humanoid robot loomed behind him, glinting with fresh paint. This bot had potential. Even this far away, Roman could appreciate the build. The hydraulic tubes attached to the limbs promised powerful physical attacks, and there could be any number of weapons hidden behind the bot's visor and outer armor.

"What about one of the two new faces at the Ring?" asked the announcer. "Miss Addison Holden or Mr. Franz Eddison?"

Those seated behind the force field on higher levels let out a massive cheer, most likely spurred on by the stardust liquor, also outlawed in Icaria. The Ring always smelled faintly of the citrus after-taste when the fights were over. Roman eyed the two competitors. One of them was the hotshot everyone was talking about.

"Only the fight will determine the victor," continued the announcer. "The rules are simple. Seven robots enter and only one comes out. Our fighters keep what they kill, and we bury the rest. Are you ready for a rooo-battle?"

The crowd erupted with energy and the hexagonal chain around the ring lifted slightly for the robots to pass beneath. Roman slid his sphere in like a bowling ball. Using the Pada taped to his forearm, he navigated it to the very center of the ring and waited for the starting bell.

"Come here to play ball?" Franz taunted Roman across the arena.

Franz dressed like every other sunkisser. Worn in Icaria, his clothes would have showed off wealth and status. His shirt's diamond pattern probably turned a lot of heads. The golden necklace probably won him a lot of attention. Some famous inventor probably designed the sleek controller in his hands. None of it mattered here. None of it would protect him. The way Franz's mouth dripped with attitude, he'd be better off wearing an Icaria enforcer's shield than jewelry.

"I wouldn't mind an easy opponent," Franz added to Addison, causing her to chuckle. Her bot pecked at the ground like its real-life inspiration. Its wings glistened. Each feather was a sharp and deadly blade.

Roman ignored them, keeping his eyes on the robots. Besides these two sunkissers, there was at least one more from Icaria, based on the university jacket drowning his small frame. His blocky robot sputtered across the floor, and he slapped the controller in his hands until the robot stopped. The other three robots in the arena were classic junkyard dogs. Bots thrown together with scraps, nothing made to match, and weapons crudely welded to the top. All but one of the fighters offered Roman a nod and kept their bots away from his sphere, knowing what it was capable of.

Canon adjusted the strap around his neck to better position his controller in front of him. The updates to the controller were as noticeable as the upgrades to his robot. He had given Roman his first loss, taught Roman how bad defeat tasted when it happened in front of several hundred people. Roman loved watching Canon's robots fall apart once he figured out how to beat them.

After their last fight, when Roman obliterated Canon's bot into a smear of char, he heard Canon muttering something about knowing how to finally beat him. Roman wondered what new secret weapon Canon had stashed under the hatch but wasn't scared. Despite the matching tires and new paint job, Roman knew a junkyard dog when he saw one.

Even when Roman had first started fighting, he hadn't dared use such crappy builds. He fetched only the nicest things from the junk piles, and after he taught himself coding, he looked for the best electronics, ripping circuits from microwaves and the control boards of TV monitors. He hadn't entered the Ring until he was sure he stood a chance. It took a year and three demolished bots before he built his sphere.

The display board above the Ring flashed, and a countdown timer replaced the rankings board. Three seconds to go.

A siren screeched throughout the building when the countdown hit zero, and the robots pounced on each other. The three junkyard dogs quickly advanced on the three sunkisser bots. Addison's bot deftly hopped away from crushing blows and quick rushes. Franz's bot fired red lasers from its eyes and flattened the control box of one of the dogs with its fists, taking it out of commission. The arena flashed red after the victory. The university kid's robot was slung into the chain barrier by one of the dogs and broke apart in a flash of sparks.

Roman yawned. He could let the carnage continue or end it. No matter the length of the fight, he'd get his scratch either way. The dogs had their fun. The remains of the blocky bot would be a decent payout to one of them, but now it was his turn. He tapped his Pada and his sphere rotated. The other fighters didn't notice until it whistled a sharp noise as the velocity increased. The blue lights under the platform dimmed slightly. The chain fence groaned.

"Finally come to play?" Franz asked. His bot's visor turned red before firing a laser. The beam ricocheted off the sphere and dissolved against the forcefield on the other side of the arena. Roman's bot kept spinning. "What a lame robot. Some king you turned out to be."

Before Roman could prove him wrong, Canon's bot rushed toward his sphere, its new tires squealing. Roman welcomed the challenge and spread his arms, staring him down. An antenna emerged from the robot's hatch and lowered into a battering ram pointed at Roman's sphere. Green sparks shot out of the antenna and singed the arena's floor, marring Roman's four-pointed crown.

"I'm taking your crown," Canon said before commanding his bot to charge into Roman's.

The green sparks intensified after touching the sphere, and several of the fighters turned their heads away from the brightness. The sphere kept spinning, unphased by the cattle prod jabbing into it. A tiny row of five lights flickered along its side. As the sphere's speed increased, the antenna snapped and flew across the arena. Roman forced his sphere into the junkyard dog. Upon impact, Canon's bot sailed across the arena, joining the heap of parts left over from the university kid's bot.

"Try harder next time," Roman taunted Canon before returning his attention to Franz and his humanoid robot.

Franz tapped his controller, and his bot approached the sphere now that the junkyard dog was out of the way. The humanoid bot raised its foot, ready to attack. Roman quickly tapped on his Pada, the digital screen flicking from a blue *up* arrow to a red *down* arrow. Franz's kick connected, but neither robot moved. Franz frantically pushed the knobs on his controller, but his bot didn't react.

Roman laughed as the crowd quieted. Everyone's attention turned to the stalemate between the two robots. Franz cursed as his refused to follow orders. The humanoid bot remained stuck as if the sphere had turned into a giant magnet. Roman slammed his palm against his Pada, initiating his finishing blow.

The fence pressed toward the center of the ring. The anti-gravity stations under the arena sputtered. Their glowing blue lights flickered wildly. The entire floor dropped several feet. Addison yelled in surprise. The remaining lights on Roman's sphere lit up. Pieces of broken robot flew into his sphere and stuck to its patchwork casing. The robots were powerless as their metal parts snapped under the intense pressure, condensing and cracking, and flying into the sphere. Oil poured from them. Sparks crashed to the floor. Franz's humanoid bot crumbled to a knee before snapping apart at the waist.

The arena sunk several more feet until Roman turned off his sphere. The platform heaved as the anti-gravity beams returned to their normal output and the ring raised to its starting position. His sphere spun around several times until all the broken parts slid off its chrome exterior. There wasn't a scratch on it.

The lower sections of the crowd erupted with noise. Their cheers ricocheted off the domed walls and ceiling. Roman's name flashed across the display board, and the spotlights illuminated the mess of robots on the arena floor. The Ring filled with voices chanting his name. Roman allowed his ego to surge at the sound of it. At times like these, he felt more like a god than a king.

Addison dropped to her knees as if the battle had drained her as much as her bot. Oil stained her blue dress and a runaway spark seared one of the sleeves. Franz, on the other side of the arena, did not look as defeated. He dropped his controller to the floor and curled his hands into fists, preparing to slug someone in the mouth. Roman sneered at him, wishing there wasn't a graveyard of robots between them. Beating sunkissers at the Ring was pleasurable, but nothing would compare with actual violence. A vein pulsed on Franz's forehead.

"Well now," the announcer said over the speakers before he hopped up a flight of hovering stairs and into the arena. Mr. O'Neal used to fight every week until he started calling the matches. Roman had watched Mr. O'Neal's robots bop and sock every challenger for years. It was a shame the old man retired before Roman could fight him. "Seems to be a quick fight tonight, ladies and gents. How are we feeling?"

The crowd was torn between shouts of triumph and demands for a rematch.

"Illegal tech?" Mr. O'Neal repeated one of the complaints he picked out of the shouting. "There can't be such a thing here. If it's a robot and it's fighting, then it's legal for the competition."

"He didn't have to flatten everything," Addison said, returning to her feet and dusting off her skirt. "I just got my little bird this morning."

Roman rolled his eyes before looking at Mr. O'Neal.

"To the victor goes the spoils," Mr. O'Neal said, "and Roman's picked up quite a shopping list."

"Melt it!" Roman shouted at the announcer.

"Pardon?" Mr. O'Neal asked, his large eyes blinking behind his glasses. The university kid shouted his distaste at Roman's wishes.

"Melt all of it."

"But, Roman." Mr. O'Neal covered the microphone with his hand. "There's a lot of cryptens in these bots. Flattened or not, you really want to—"

"I said melt them," Roman repeated, locking eyes with Franz, who looked like he could catch fire from his anger. If the sunkissers wanted to come down here and throw their scratch away in ill-prepared robot battles, he'd make sure nothing was left. "Send the slag to my prep room."

Roman tapped his Pada and instructed his sphere to roll to him. He picked it up and turned away from the arena. The shouts of the crowd, the protests of the sunkissers, the heat of the blow torch followed him to his prep room while his Pada flashed with the deposit of tonight's winnings.

It was a good night.

Chapter Three

Roman sat in his prep room watching his cryptens almost double on his Pada screen. It did the same to the endorphins in his brain. This was more than surviving. This was living. His door slid open, and the continued chorus of his name flooded the room as Mr. O'Neal wheeled in a crate of melted metal and wires. Usually, one of the Ring's employees handled this job. Roman eyed him, placing a protective hand atop his sphere.

Mr. O'Neal shut the door and patted the top of melted slag. "Good fight tonight, Roman."

Roman powered off his Pada. "Nothing unexpected."

Mr. O'Neal chuckled. "A little humility goes a long way."

"Not down here." Roman could barely define the word. It had no place in the Slums nor for a king.

"What do you have planned for all this?" Mr. O'Neal asked about the slag. "Still seems like a waste to melt down so many good bots."

Roman stretched out his legs, making the announcer take a step back. Mr. O'Neal had always picked Roman's brain about new bots and ideas. When Roman could first afford his prep room, Mr. O'Neal spent many nights sitting beside him just to talk. It still made him uneasy. He didn't give away his ideas for free anymore.

"I've got plans." It was the only answer Roman would give. He'd find a use for the scrap.

"I can't wait to see them." The curt reply didn't seem to bother Mr. O'Neal's joyful mood. "I've got a couple friends coming over tonight. You should come too. They're big fans."

Roman didn't like fans. He liked followers. "I'm good."

"Come on, Roman," Mr. O'Neal tried again. "It'd be good for you."

Roman glared at the man. Kindness was about as rare in the Slums as a decent meal was. People didn't want the robot killer's company without wanting something else. "Why? They looking for a job?"

"No." Mr. O'Neal paled at Roman's question. "It's just nice to have people in your life."

Roman laughed. "No."

Mr. O'Neal frowned but accepted the loss. He bid farewell and left the prep room.

Roman sat alone next to his pile of melted robots. He took a pull from a glass of stardust and donned his coat. He felt alive, and he wasn't going to waste it inside his little prep room.

His victory lap around the Ring was cut short as he rounded a corner and spotted one of the sunkissers from the fight. Franz Eddison stood with two others, and none of them looked happy.

"Damn fight was rigged," one of the older sunkissers was saying. He crumbled a betting ticket in his hands. Roman didn't need to see it to know it would say loser. "No way something like that can be made down here."

"How would they rig a fight, Shaw?" asked the third one in the group. "You're just being a sore loser. Next time bet on their king and you won't feel so bad. I actually made a little money tonight."

"Don't call him that," Franz growled. He furiously swiped between digital displays on his Pada. "He's nothing but slum trash."

"Yeah, that Koa isn't a king," Shaw added. "He's just a menace. You know how many complaints I receive about him after every fight? He's always terrorizing someone or stealing something. Last month, a lady told me someone tried taking her kid. It had to be him."

Roman scrunched his nose at the idea. He was a lot of things, but he would never hurt a kid. Take their shoes, sure, but never hurt them.

"Imagine what he could do with some proper tools and parts?" the third sunkisser asked, sounding amazed with his own ideas. His friends frowned at him.

"You're dusted," Shaw said, pocketing his sheet and eyeing the man.

"Am not," he replied, but the glossy sheen of his eyes wasn't selling his lie. His breath probably smelled like a week-old orange. "Franz, what do you think? I've seen you in the labs. What kind of stuff could he build there?"

With sunkisser technology, Roman could build anything. But he didn't need their superior gadgets. He made sure everyone knew that.

Franz tuned off his Pada. Whatever data he had been reading apparently didn't please him. He tightened his hands into fists. "Doesn't matter what he built. It would only ever be slummer trash. Tonight was a fluke. Like Shaw said, fight was rigged. I'll beat him next time."

Roman couldn't remember the last sunkisser that stayed for more than a single fight against him, but he wouldn't mind if Franz did. The humanoid bot was impressive. He would like to have one that wasn't currently a pile of junk. Roman laughed, gaining all of their attention. "Whatever you have to tell yourself."

Franz stepped between Roman and the other sunkissers. His hands were still in fists. Roman welcomed the fight. He craved the violence.

"You're going to regret that," said Franz.

Roman shook his head. "I don't regret anything."

"Everyone knows I had the better bot. You cheated and I will figure out how, and you'll be banned. You'll never fight again. I'll make sure of it."

A snake-like grin split Roman's face. "They'll never stop cheering my name."

Franz shoved Roman and Roman shoved back harder, sending Franz into the wall. Roman pressed his forearm against Franz's throat.

"I might be nothing but slummer trash, but I'll always be better than you," Roman said.

Franz's response sputtered on his lips as Roman pressed harder. When his cheeks turned blue, Roman backed away.

"I'm telling my father," Franz declared after sucking down a deep breath.

"I'm so scared," Roman said. He turned to face the other sunkissers. Shaw had run off somewhere, but his dusted friend stared at Roman in either awe or terror. Roman confused the two a lot. He eyed the purple scarf hanging off the sunkisser's shoulder. "Nice scarf. Looks warm."

The man looked surprised Roman addressed him and it took him a moment to respond. "It is. It reflects body heat. I got it from—"

"Give it here," Roman interrupted, yanking it off the man before he could react. Roman stuffed it into his coat pocket. "I like your shoes, too."

They were ugly. The thin sole wouldn't last a week on the junkyard streets.

"Stop it," Franz ordered, pushing himself off the wall.

Roman asked him, "You going to stop me?"

Franz didn't respond. Roman clicked his tongue. Sunkissers were all the same: worthless, spineless thieves.

Roman finished relieving the man of his shoes and turned down the hallway. He was done messing around with these sunkissers. His victory celebration waited for him at home.

"Hey!" Franz shouted behind him, his heavy footsteps echoing off the walls.

Maybe Roman wasn't completely finished messing with them. He slid to the side, grabbed Franz's arm and spun him back around into the other sunkisser. The pair crashed to the ground in a tangled mess of limbs and designer clothes.

Roman tossed the ugly shoes into a trash can and laughed his way out of the Ring.

Roman ground his teeth together, staring at the line of white chrome Icarian carriages parked outside the Ring. His undeniable victory over the rich kids should have satisfied him for at least the night, but anger heated the skin under his collar. He tapped his tattooed fingers against his sphere tucked under his arm.

One carriage had turquoise tires. He was willing to bet all his winnings it belonged to Addison. He was also willing to bet the color was her only personality trait. The rest of her was likely sucked dry by the ease of living above the acid clouds. Roman doubted she or the other two city kids had ever experienced a rain shower. Experienced the burns that covered the slummers who were unfortunate enough to be caught in one. Icaria kept the Slums covered for the most part, but it didn't stop every drop.

The other carriages were standard in their onion-shape design except for the one parked at the end of the line. Its oblong shape and tinted windows angered him the most, and he wanted to toss his sphere under it and destroy it.

The license plate bore the last name of the carriage's owner: Flint.

Roman hadn't seen the name since he was a child. Since the Flint family left the Slums. Without him.

He was used to rage. He was used to the fire lacing his veins whenever he encountered the sunkissers. He was used to going out of his way to make their time in the Slums as miserable as possible. Roman was not used to the heaviness that currently gripped him. He felt bolted to the ground as the license plate filled his vision. His insides shook with the need for action, but he was unable to move. He had written off the Flints the day they left. If they chose to leave him for dead, then they were dead to him as well. But if their carriage was here, then so were they, and Roman didn't believe in ghosts.

"Hey man." Scrap joined him and yanked Roman free. Once he regained control of his body, Roman spat on the sidewalk. "Thanks for waiting," Scrap continued, not noticing Roman's episode. "Got my registration finished, and I'm ready to go. Gotta get the oil leak figured out, but that's a tomorrow job. Let's go celebrate!"

"See that carriage?" Roman popped Scrap's joyful mood, pointing with his free hand.

Scrap squinted until he found the one in question. "Yeah, what about it?"

"I want tabs on it and its occupants at all times." Roman didn't look away from the carriage. The last name seared his brain. He rolled his shoulders as more imaginary chains tried weighing him down.

"I've got just the guy—"

"No," Roman interrupted. "I need you to do it."

"But Ro?"

Roman forced his eyes off the license plate and looked at Scrap. Motor oil stained his cheek like a permanent bruise. Roman hadn't realized how much Scrap had grown since he found him in a trash pile, forgotten like the rest of the junk. Roman also hadn't realized how much he trusted Scrap. It wasn't a lot, but it was enough to give him this job. "Do this for me, Scrap. I'll give you your extra ten percent."

Scrap smiled. "And a free tune-up on my arm?"

"Fine. Just do it."

Chapter Four

Roman sneered across the scrap metal table, his expression as sharp as the jagged edges, and pressed his fist against the surface. His knuckles were sticky with blood. Stamped impressions of fists cover the table. His four-pointed crown was carved in a corner nearest him. Neon lights bounced off every part of the bar and were periodically broken up by swiveling overhead lights that were helpful in disorienting his patrons.

"Come on already," Roman challenged the man seated across from him. "I'm getting bored."

The other man was cut from the same slum-stained cloth as Roman, but he didn't wear the filth as well. This man was just a rat, scurrying through the trash where Roman ruled over it. The man aimed a sharpened silver coin at Roman's fist, so when flung across the table it'd cut into Roman's third and most damaged knuckle.

The man fired the coin, and it embedded between Roman's fist and the table. Roman didn't flinch. Blood oozed out of his knuckle and soaked the coin. Three strikes to the same bleeding finger usually knocked the strongest player off their seat, but not Roman.

He dug the coin out of his skin and positioned it on the table while the man readied his fist the same way Roman had. Welts of healed flesh grimaced on all four of the man's knuckles. A terrible purple color tarnished his right-most finger. Roman turned the coin slightly so one of its sharpened curves pointed directly at the damaged digit.

Onlookers placed more coins on the side of the table and made their bets. The archaic money system existed in the Slums as a backup in case their Padas failed to establish a connection to Icaria and their banks. The untraceable coins were the perfect scratch for betting on bar games. They were small, easy to spend, easy to cut up for extra fun, and easier to pocket when left unattended.

Roman flicked the coin across the table as swiftly as a blade. It cut into the man's fists just like one, too, and lodged between flesh and bone. The man howled, clutching his hand close to his chest. Roman smiled; his grin as bloody as the game. The flesh and blood-covered coin clattered to the table as it fell from the man's hand. A shot of illegally made stardust appeared beside Roman. He pocketed his winnings out of habit. He slammed his drink out of want. He eyed his next conquest out of boredom.

Roman wanted to fill his night with distractions until Scrap returned with his report. He wanted to stay so busy he wouldn't find the Flints himself and show them what leaving him in the Slums had done. He wanted to prove how wrong they had been about him. He wanted to show off how important he had become here without being force-fed by Icarian silver spoons.

"Got a call for you, boss," the waitress who delivered his shot said on her return trip from the bar. Her serving tray was another piece of old-world scrap metal. A black 55 was stamped in the center. Her dark gloves protected her hands from the sign's rough edges.

"I'm busy." Roman didn't lift his gaze from a pair of women giggling and sharing a glass of stardust at a table across the room. The lipstick stains on the two straws changed orange to green under the neon lights. Roman thought if they could share a drink that strong, then they should be able to share him, too.

"It's Scrap." The waitress held out a brick-shaped device with two speakers fitted on either end.

Roman snapped his attention to the waitress, grabbed the phone, and waved her away.

"What's the word?" Roman asked into the device, turning his back to the nearest patron, a kid as skinny as barstool legs who'd spent most of the night looking for crumbs.

"There's just one guy," Scrap answered, his voice scratchy on the other end of the line. The technology was outdated even by the Slums' standards, but it kept anyone from tapping into the transmission. "A fella around our age. He's been roaming around looking for something."

Out of habit, Roman raised a knuckle to his mouth and bit it. The rust flavor knocked loose a few thoughts he'd rather not have. "Not someone?"

"Could be, but who would a sunkisser know down here? Guy's probably looking for something he threw away." Scrap laughed at his joke.

"I paid you to follow him," Roman growled, anger burning through the pain Scrap's comment caused. "Not for your ideas."

"Sorry, Ro." Scrap didn't sound offended by Roman's remarks. The mechanic had become familiar with Roman's sharp edges.

"Where's he at now?"

"Headed your way, actually," Scrap answered. "About to turn down the street to Dead Dove."

Roman stood. The people sitting on his left flinched at his sudden movement.

"Follow him in, but don't engage," he told Scrap before ending the call.

Roman sauntered across the room to his waitress, placing a hand on her back and leaning down to whisper in her ear, "I have a guest arriving. Send him to the back."

"Him?" the waitress asked before adjusting her question. "How will I know who?"

"Trust me, you'll know." Roman straightened. "And no interruptions once he's here, understand?"

"Understood, boss."

"Hey, Roman," the man the waitress was delivering food to slurred Roman's name. Whatever was in his cup gave him an unhealthy boost of confidence. "You getting your robot out or what? Thing looks so tiny at the Ring. Hard to believe it's been winning so much. Did one of them dust runners smuggle something for you?"

Roman frowned. Half of the man's words were interrupted by hiccups and the other half were drenched in a rancid stench.

"Listen Donny," the waitress started, but Roman raised a hand to silence them both.

"He's done," Roman told them. Based on his state, Donny probably spent all he had already, but Roman's pride wasn't something he'd lay aside for any amount of cryptens. "Get him out of here."

"You heard the boss." The waitress tugged Donny up by his elbow.

The man slid out of her grasp and planted his butt back in his chair. "Don't be like that Tansy. Least let me finish my food."

Tansy yanked the platter of deep-fried mushrooms off the table, holding it high above her head. Roman had always liked her willingness to step into a fight. The sides of her blonde hair were shaved, showing off a speckling of tattooed stars along her scalp. The day she got them, she asked Roman if he thought they were cool. He'd never told her that he did, or that the hatch-lined star tattooed on his elbow was for her.

"You're done," Tansy said.

Donny wasn't convinced. He laid a disgusting hand against her hip and squeezed. Tansy stiffened for a moment, her eyes widening before fear replaced the shock. Roman didn't hesitate. He bashed his boot into Donny's stomach, knocking him off the stool with a mighty crash.

Every head in the bar turned to watch the scene, but no one offered to get between Roman and his prey.

Roman grabbed Donny's wrist and launched him toward the door. A loud snarl from Roman spurred Donny out of Dead Dove.

"Thanks boss," Tansy told him after Donny was gone, one hand rubbing the spot he'd touched, "but I could've handled it."

"I know." Roman stole a piece of food from the platter. Mushrooms were one of the few foods that could grow in their dark world, and Roman squished the deep-fried fungus between his teeth before swallowing. "But I wanted to. Don't forget, no interruptions."

"Roger." Tansy nodded, but then added, "What should I do with these?"

Roman eyed the mushrooms. He knew he should eat them, he hadn't eaten since that morning, but the same queasy feeling he always felt before a fight was bubbling in his gut. "Donny pay for them yet?"

"Of course," Tansy answered. "Take the cryptens first, that was your number one rule when I started, or did you forget?"

Roman never forgot, he just didn't always trust his staff not to get soft. Roman pointed at the skinny kid lurking behind a table of customers and called him over.

"Your hands work?" Roman asked him.

"Yes sir," the boy answered. He didn't look at Roman, his gaze settling on the still-steaming plate of food on Tansy's tray.

"If you pick up all the trash outside Dead Dove, you can have this," Roman said.

The boy quickly accepted the deal and bolted to the exit to get started. Roman appreciated the kid's eagerness; it was the same he had when he first started his business for other slummers, but he wasn't the one people called to clean up trash. People only called Roman when there was something much messier to deal with. Tasks that would really dirty their hands.

A small smile tugged at the side of Tansy's mouth. "Want me to warm them back up after he's done?"

"Depends on how good a job he does."

Roman weaved his way to the back of the bar. He grabbed a tin can of stardust from under the bar's counter and vanished behind the door marked with his four-pointed crown. Dead Dove was a long building that stretched into a series of old shipping containers fashioned together to make an office, workshop, and living space. He handled the books for Dead Dove in the office, his tech in the workshop, and handled himself in the other space.

His office was as sordid as his bar. Red neon lights ran the length of the wall casting an eerie glow on the ceiling and bathing the black furniture in a crimson hue. The room wasn't designed to entertain guests, and Roman relished in that discomfort. Only one chair sat at the desk, cabinets made from welded scrap metal hung crookedly on the wall, a cracked TV hummed with electricity, and the wires connecting it to a glowing power source hissed. Hidden below a hatch on the floor was a collection of weapons that Roman kept looking for excuses to use.

Roman sipped the stardust, careful the tin's lid didn't cut his lips, and sat in the chair. The alcohol sloshed into his stomach, and he felt his blood thicken. He needed to be calm when Oliver Flint saw him. He needed to be a king.

A knock echoed off the office door before Oliver Flint was pushed inside. He stumbled, his shiny shoes catching against the raised doorframe, and then pitched forward and slammed into the desk. He splayed both hands on the desktop to stop his fall. The door shut and Oliver looked up, taking an eternity to lift his eyes to meet Roman's.

Heat gripped Roman's neck. He didn't see Oliver Flint as he was now, as a rich sunkisser with tanned skin and rounded cheeks who probably hadn't missed a meal in a decade, but as the ruddy-faced boy who used to build robots with him in the junkyards. The ruddy-faced boy who left in an Icarian carriage the second they called him. The ruddy-faced boy who left Roman in the Slums with the piles of trash.

"Roman," Oliver breathed like he was relieved to see him. "Roman, is that really you?"

"Don't recognize me?" Roman hissed.

Oliver smiled. His teeth were straight. His entire face lit up. "I've been looking for you all night. I waited at the Ring after your fight, but you never came out of your prep room. It's good to see you, *filos*."

"It's awful to see you."

Oliver's smile faltered for a second, and he said quietly, "Come on, Ro. Don't be like that."

"Be like what?" Roman shoved away from the desk, away from Oliver, and stood. The stardust tin rattled, and golden liquid spilled over the rim and stained the documents underneath it. "What'd you expect I'd be after all this time?"

"Happy to see me." Oliver straightened and matched Roman's height as best he could, but the difference hadn't changed. Roman still had a head on him.

"You left me."

Roman snatched the collar of Oliver's well-made suit and gripped the white material. The embroidered logo of some laboratory crumpled under the force. He wanted to hit him. He wanted to pound ten years of feeling worthless into his skull.

Oliver placed a hand over Roman's fist to pull him off, and Roman flinched as if the physical contact burned. He tightened his grip around Oliver's collar. Blood from his open knuckles leached onto the fabric.

"You know that wasn't my choice!" Oliver sucked in a shallow breath. "You know my parents made that decision. It was our ticket out of here. It was Liza's only chance at surviving."

Roman choked on his rage-filled breath. People got sick in the Slums all the time, but he never saw someone get as sick as Liza. Roman tried protecting her as best he could, but he couldn't help her fight off an illness no matter how much of his food he gave her. "Did she?"

"Yeah, Liza's okay now," Oliver answered. "She spent a year in the hospital up there. Had to get a new lung, but she's better."

"Is she here too?" Roman let go of Oliver's shirt. He couldn't picture her seated inside Dead Dove. He refused to think of people like Donny getting her in their sights.

Oliver shook his head, rubbing his hand around his throat. "No, but I know she'd love to see you. Maybe just not like this."

Oliver gestured to Roman and his grime-slick arms, his bloodied knuckles, his split eyebrow, his tattoos, his anger.

"I'd never hurt your sister." Roman tossed himself back into his chair, rattling everything on his desk. He kicked the side of it. He was losing control of the situation he was supposed to own.

"Do you want to restart this conversation?"

"No," Roman answered in a bitter tone. "What are you doing back in the Slums? I doubt your dad wants you rolling in the filth again."

"You're right about that. I'm here on business." Oliver looked around the office. "Is there another place to sit?"

"Not enough chairs thrown out. You sunkissers are too busy sitting in them doing nothing." Roman snickered at his joke.

Oliver frowned. "Icaria isn't like that. And don't call me a sunkisser."

"I wouldn't know what that city is like," Roman said.

"You could come with me and—"

Roman slammed his boot on the floor. "Not for all the scratch in the world."

"Not even if I asked you to?"

"Not for all the guilt in your body."

"Guilt?" Oliver sucked in a breath.

Roman rolled his eyes. "You ain't going to pull me up there now because you feel bad about leaving me when we were kids. I've got things here. I'm a king."

Oliver raised an eyebrow, glancing around the office. "It's quite a kingdom."

"Sorry it's not painted gold, but this is what the real world looks like, sunkisser." Roman pulled the tin of stardust closer to him. He shouldn't need to prove himself to Oliver or any sunkisser. His name atop the Ring's scoreboard should do that. The cryptens in his account should do that. His bar, the cleanest in all the Slums with working stardust drafts and an actual kitchen, should do that. But it didn't keep Roman from wanting to show off more. He resisted the urge to open his Pada and show Oliver all the people who needed him. "What business do you need done? I won't offer any discounts because you knew me once."

"I'm not here to buy a drink," Oliver said, confused. "This is serious."

"I'm serious too. What do you need done? Someone owe you money? Someone steal something? Does someone need to disappear?"

"Roman, what have you been doing here?" Oliver's eyes widened, but his concern didn't penetrate Roman's thick skin.

"Whatever I need to do to survive," he snarled.

Oliver didn't look frightened like Roman expected him to. "Good, because this is definitely something to keep you surviving."

Roman took another sip of the stardust and waited for Oliver to continue.

"President Hinge sent me to look for anyone with a talent for tech, like how they found me. He wants to bring up people with a knack for it. Enroll them in the university." Oliver tapped his manicured fingers against the desk. "It's a community project."

"It sounds like a slaughterhouse."

"To elevate people to Icaria?" Oliver crossed his arms, tucking his fingers under his armpits.

"What do your people want with my people?"

"*Your people?*"

"Answer the question, Oliver." Roman demanded. Oliver hadn't changed enough in ten years to lose his tell. He still fidgeted with his fingers whenever he lied. "What's really going on here? The only charity sunkissers do for us is not flushing their shit on our roofs."

"Why can't you believe me?" Oliver asked. "You used to."

"When we were ten. When we were supposed to be building a robot fighter together. That is, before Icaria offered to buy your code and you sold out our whole operation."

It was a crappy operation that no one but them had believed in, but it had given Roman something to hold on to. He thought Oliver had felt the same way. Roman could see it: both their names would be up in lights every night as they became champions of the Ring with their junkyard dog.

Roman had followed through with their vision without his partner.

"Roman," Oliver sighed. "Please. I wanted to stay, or at least take you with me, but it wasn't the deal. Icaria didn't want—"

"Didn't want me," Roman grumbled. "They didn't want the kid who found the parts in their trash. Just the kid who rigged them all together."

"Looks like you proved them wrong, though." Oliver grinned. "I did see your match tonight. I've seen the recordings of others, too. What is that bot of yours? How'd you program it to access the gravity stations under the arena? It was slanting brilliant."

Roman refused to let Oliver's compliment go to his head. He forced his lips to stay in a straight line despite them wanting to hitch up in a smile. He *was* slanting brilliant, and it was about time people took notice.

"If your school is wanting kids, why are you asking me to go?" Roman asked. "And don't say it's because of our history."

"Okay, you want it straight. I respect that." Oliver ran a hand through his blond hair. He wore it shorter now; the curls clung close to his head rather than hanging past his ears. "President Hinge is looking for a solution to a problem in Icaria."

"So, it *is* a slaughterhouse."

"Jeez, Roman, will you listen?"

Roman waved for Oliver to continue.

"We're looking for new ideas. President Hinge believes we've hit a wall and wants a new perspective."

"The only perspective we know here is the underside of Icaria."

Oliver ignored him and continued, "That's where the education comes in. Cultivate and help develop talents down here."

"You're looking for another golden boy."

"Yes," Oliver answered.

Roman set a bloody knuckle against his teeth. He didn't need to be in Icaria to know how advanced their university was. If building the ultimate robot fighter was his goal, he'd be an idiot to pass up an opportunity to elevate. Even if just to get new parts. Even if just to get a decent meal. The shipping fees to get anything new out of Icaria were so high, only a few slummers could afford it. Roman could stock up there and bring it all back with him. It was too easy, and, unlike the rats in the Slums, he could smell a trap.

"You never said what the problem is."

"I can't," Oliver answered. "I'm not allowed to discuss it."

"Not even with a friend?" Roman grinned, but it felt more like a sneer.

"You haven't been too friendly," Oliver said.

Roman crossed his arms. "You said this problem affects my survival."

Oliver nodded. "It does."

"Then start talking or start signing my death certificate."

Oliver sighed. He turned toward the door and Roman feared he was about to walk out of his life again, but Oliver paced the room instead. Roman hated how he saw his best friend in the body of this should-be stranger. Oliver had paced this same way when they were kids, when he couldn't figure out a string of code, turning on his heel into a tiny spin when he reached the end of the room. He stopped abruptly and snapped just as he would have ten years ago.

"I'll show you," Oliver said. "I can't tell you, but if you're smart enough to figure it out then it won't matter."

"Smart enough?" Roman would take any opportunity to prove to Oliver Flint, to all the sunkissers, that he was better than them. "I'll figure out your stupid puzzle with my eyes closed."

Chapter Five

Roman announced his return to the bar by slamming the door against the wall. Scrap turned away from Tansy and stared at Roman and Oliver, his eyes wanting answers that Roman wasn't ready to share. Scrap and Tansy sat at the bar together, their bodies close, a single beer between them. Some nights, the three of them ended the night like that, sitting together and talking about nothing. Roman never sat as close to them as they did with each other, though. Scrap's gaze darted between Roman and Oliver. All the patrons' gazes drifted to Oliver. The sunkisser was an eyesore to the bar, his white coat becoming a vomit bucket of colors as the neon lights fell across it.

Roman left Oliver to stand in the open and joined his employees at the bar. He wanted Oliver to know that no matter how easy his life was in Icaria, it wouldn't make things simple or pretty here. Roman still kept an ear toward the front of the room in case someone tried something funny.

"No free drinks," Roman said to Scrap and Tansy.

"I paid," Scrap defended. "Running an errand?"

"Yeah." Roman answered their coded message. An errand was a job, and even though Oliver swore he didn't have one for him, Roman knew better than to believe anything he said. Icaria had changed Oliver's outward appearance so much it wouldn't have been a surprise if his insides changed too.

Scrap nodded. "Got it."

Tansy rose from her chair, taking Roman's empty stardust can behind the counter and dunking it in the semi-clean washing bin. "Be careful."

That was the end of the exchange. Like the hundreds of jobs before, Scrap knew his duties. If Roman didn't send word in twelve hours, then he was to assume the worst. Scrap got first pick of Dead Dove and anything useful he could find in the back. If Scrap was smart, he'd salvage the bar and run it himself, but Roman knew Scrap better than that. He had more metal on his brain than in his prosthetic arm and would be drawn to the workshop like a rat to poison.

If Tansy kept proving herself to him, Roman considered leaving part of Dead Dove to her. She'd be able to run the place well enough. This bar was always waiting for him in the past because of her, and he knew she'd be able to fight off any vultures that tried to take it. Roman tapped his knuckles against the bar top before turning back to Oliver, who had been dragged into a conversation with a bar fly Roman hadn't squashed yet.

The Up-Lifter rested her hand on Oliver's arm as he answered her questions. He spoke quickly and awkwardly, trying to pull himself out of her reach, but she kept leaning in. The yellow robes the group used to wear were rare these days, but members still sported the color in handkerchiefs or scarves around their necks.

"Tell me more," she cooed. Roman could smell the stardust on her breath even from his position. "Is the sky truly made of diamonds?"

"Just gases," Oliver answered. "Nitrogen and oxygen, mostly."

"What are their colors?"

"Pardon?" Oliver tried stepping back again, but her grip on his arm tightened.

"Are they yellow like the sun?" she snapped.

"They're gasses. They don't have colors."

The Up-Lifter yanked her hand away from Oliver like it pained her to touch him. "Liar! Blasphemy! You say you're from the sky but don't know the truth of it."

"But they really don't," Oliver tried to soothe her, but she continued to shriek.

"Cut it, Janee," Roman said.

"It's Star Seer," she corrected him, crossing her arms and straightening in her seat.

Roman rolled his eyes. He thought the Up-Lifters stopped renaming themselves after the final failed attempt to ascend, but some members must have held on to the beliefs tighter than others. It didn't bother him. As long as she kept paying her tab, she could call herself whatever she wanted.

Roman kicked Oliver's boot and nodded toward the exit. Oliver was happy to follow him out of Dead Dove.

"My carriage is around the corner," Oliver said after they exited the bar. He tightened his coat around his frame trying to ward off the ever-present chill of the Slums.

"Forget how to walk?" Roman slipped his hands into his pockets and started down the sidewalk. The area outside Dead Dove was free of trash. Even a strip of metal embedded into the pavement had been yanked free. The skinny kid had earned his meal.

Oliver matched Roman's pace. "It'd be quicker to drive."

"On these roads? Doubt it."

"If you can even call them roads." Oliver's steps were almost a march as he avoided the grime. The hem of his coat was already stained.

"We get by just fine." Roman smashed an aluminum can under his boot. "Where are we going?"

"A grav-quadrant," Oliver answered, flicking on his Pada. It was so dinky compared to the one Roman taped against his forearm. At first glance, Roman had mistaken it for a watch, but as Oliver turned it on, a hologram screen appeared above his wrist. His face reflected the soft green light as he worked the interface. "Closest one is E-14."

"You have a grid of the Slums?" Roman had never heard of his home referred to by quadrants before. "Of course you do, spending all your time looking down on us."

"The grid system was established before I got there." Bitterness salted Oliver's words. "Go south."

Roman led the way, only slowing down when Oliver consulted his Pada and directed him down a new alley. Tubes of neon lighting snaked across buildings, twisting into letters advertising some of the building's offerings. Most spelled "stay out." Mounds of trash rose in the distance like a picturesque hillside. A curtain of acid rain fell around the border of the Slums, dissolving anything on the other side. The chrome underside of Icaria hovered above them like an umbrella. The neon lights reflected by its metal belly were the closest thing to sunshine Roman knew.

"Did the Up-Lifters change their rules?" Oliver asked after a while.

"Rules about what?" Roman kept walking.

"Stardust," Oliver clarified. "I thought they weren't allowed to drink it. Didn't your mom say it would weigh them down and they wouldn't be able to ascend?"

"Do you still think people can float out of here?" Roman snapped.

Oliver didn't respond.

The Up-Lifters' beliefs were foolish, and Roman hated that he knew them all. A religion born from the filth, it was just a bunch of lies. People paid the High Riser in food, cryptens, favors, whatever they could to ensure they would ascend with him. Evan as a kid, Roman had known people didn't leave the Slums.

Unless they were the Flint family.

Roman kicked a piece of trash hard, and it exploded into a cloud of moths and flies.

Oliver's Pada directed them to a lifeless section on the edge of the Slums. Hazy fog from the rain danced along the ground. Roman adjusted the collar of his jacket to protect the back of his neck.

No one dared to live this close to the edge. Without Icaria's unintentional protection, acid rain would melt away flesh like tissue paper. When the rain did pause, some slummers ventured out looking for a better life than the one provided in the junkyard. Either they found it, or the rain came back, because Roman never saw anyone return. In the Slums, there were only two options: live in the junkyard or live in a graveyard.

"How's your mom?" Oliver tried for conversation again.

"Dead."

Oliver gasped. "I'm so sorry."

"Why?" Roman was close to snapping again. "You didn't deny her medicine. That was Icaria."

Even as a boy, Roman realized how much his mother's treatment would cost. He knew they didn't have the cryptens to cover it; even if Roman worked every day for ten years he'd never scrounge up enough. Icaria could have saved his mother, could have saved a lot of people, but their greed was too important. Roman had learned the value of human life that day. He'd learned that compassion would get him nothing but heartache.

"How long ago?"

"Doesn't matter. Won't bring her back." Roman slowed as the pathway forked. "Which way?"

"Ro, if I knew . . . Listen . . . I'm—"

Roman stopped his useless rambling. "Which way, Flint?"

Oliver checked his map. "Left one."

They continued in silence and approached a ten-foot-tall fence encircling a stone building in the center of a gravel lot. A large antenna rose from the roof. Blue energy hummed between the top of the antenna and the underside of Icaria, still several hundred feet above.

"I forgot how dark it is," Oliver admitted, looking around. The gravitational energy was the only light, and it created too many shadows to be useful. As the energy moved, so did the shadows. Everything expanded and contracted like an erratic breath.

Roman ducked under a rip in the fencing. "Got too used to the sunshine, golden boy?"

"I don't know if I'll ever get used to it," Oliver answered, following Roman through the fence and past *the no trespassing* sign hanging on the side. "It's nothing like we were told. The brightness of it. The warmth of it. If it didn't burn my eyes, I'd stare at it forever."

"Sounds awful."

"I'm sure you'll change your mind when you see it."

Roman didn't respond. His boots crunched against the gravel as they neared the gravity station. There were over two dozen of these glorified magnets in the Slums with the sole purpose of keeping Icaria suspended at cloud level, above the acid rain. In the early years, Icarian enforcers guarded the stations until they couldn't stomach the smell, or so Roman had been told. Now everything was automated, and Icaria didn't guard the only connection point between them and the Slums. There wasn't a need when the gravity beams did it for them. Roman peered through the viewing window on the station's door. It was empty.

"This it?" Roman asked. A few lights blinked on the monitoring station against a wall. The room looked as lifeless as this quadrant of the Slums. Roman couldn't even see signs of rodents. The dusty floor was free of their footprints.

When Oliver didn't respond, Roman turned and found him staring up. Horror froze him in place. Roman grabbed Oliver's chin and yanked his head down.

"Don't act like you didn't know about it," Roman barked, releasing Oliver and stepping away.

He didn't need to look at the dead bodies suspended in the gravity field generated by the antenna to know what spooked Oliver. Every slummer had grown used to the image. The bodies circled the beam like discarded satellites. Their yellow robes trailed behind them like a comet's tail. Once sucked into the field, the air was pulled from their lungs. In the early years, the Up-Lifters thought they could climb up to Icaria. They thought they could use the gravity beam like a ladder. They thought wrong.

Oliver's voice shook. "I didn't. I didn't know."

"Best not to look." Roman shoved Oliver toward the door, wanting to get out from under the bodies in case one decided to return to the Slums. "Is this it?"

"Yeah." Oliver peered inside the window, his voice hollow.

A wild arc of blue energy cracked away from the beam and disappeared, vanishing high above. Something large and metallic groaned in response. Roman crossed his arms and tried to see past Oliver's head, but the window wasn't made for two people.

"Well, what do you see?" he asked impatiently. "Why are we out here?"

"Look here." Oliver stepped aside and ushered Roman forward. "Over on the left, the gauge next to the reading logs. See it?"

"Yeah. What about it?" Roman cupped his hands around his eyes to better see inside the gloom.

"You'll have to figure that out. I can't tell you," Oliver reminded.

Roman cursed and pulled away from the window. "You dragged me all this way to show me a stupid read-out?"

"I offered to drive us."

Oliver had never been afraid to challenge Roman when they were kids. Roman found a little comfort in seeing at least that hadn't changed.

"Whatever." Roman tried the doorknob, but it was locked.

The gravity beam seized with energy again and bathed the landscape in blue. Several tiny arms of energy dropped to the ground and scorched wherever they touched. The smell of burning rubber filled the air. Spiderwebs of blue light imprinted the ground before fading away.

Roman stared at the gravity and the bodies drifting around it. The blue light the gravity stations produced was as hazy as the fog when seen from the center of the Slums. There was no telling how long the beam had been misfiring like this. It crackled as more currents seized inside, branching the beam apart like a lightning strike. "Let me guess, that ain't normal."

"No, it isn't."

Two more arcs touched down around them, liftings Roman's hair with static. A coil of energy broke off and ran across the top of the fence several meters before rejoining the energy arc. The whole arc snapped back into the beam with a thunderous crash. Blue sparks showered against the ground.

Roman kicked the doorknob.

"What are you doing?" Oliver shrieked, the property damage startling him more than the energy storming around them.

"I'm not standing in the open like this." Roman smashed his heel against the door until it opened. "I'll wait out the storm in here."

Roman entered the station, walking into a cobweb, and gagged on the room's musky odor. He'd smelled garbage piles nicer than this place. Another energy blast left a black scar on the land outside, and Oliver followed him, covering his nose and mouth with his hand to block the smell. The ground sizzled, and little electric fingers snaked toward the station. Roman propped the door back into place. Sporadic blue light flashed through the tiny window. Roman felt like it was taunting him. The flashing light looking like a nasty smile snapping its teeth in laughter.

Oliver tapped on his Pada and used the interface's glow to light the room. He examined the automated displays on the monitors, writing their readings on the Pada's screen. Roman set a scabbed knuckle against his teeth as he watched Oliver move from screen to screen, tapping on some of the dials and typing on the keyboards of others. Roman gritted his teeth. He hated not knowing what Oliver was doing, or what he should be doing. This gravity station was on his land. Even though it was built by Icaria, Roman should still know the importance of it.

Whatever story the read outs were telling, Oliver seemed upset. After recording the data of the final gauge in his Pada, he ran a hand through his blond curls and sighed heavily. Roman stepped to the displays and leaned down to better see the gauge Oliver had first pointed out.

"Still won't tell me what all this is?" Roman's eyes darted across the board as he tried to make sense of the readings. Diagnostics had never been his strength. He used to leave the numbers and codes to Oliver while he slammed together pieces they found in the junkyard. Fastening a vacuum cleaner hose to an old motor to circulate oil made more sense than the code to start it remotely.

"I can't," Oliver answered.

"Can't or won't? It's not like anyone up there is going to know." Roman swallowed the bile bubbling up his throat. He'd never get used to Oliver picking the sunkissers over him. Again and again.

Oliver rubbed the back of his neck. The light from his Pada illuminated a tiny scar below his left ear. "Tell me what that gauge reads."

Roman almost barked his refusal to the order, but the thin line of Oliver's mouth matched the thin line of the scar too well. He didn't have that scar when he left. Roman studied the gauge. "It's the station's output power. Reading low. It's out of the green, dropping close to red."

"The one next to it?" Oliver asked.

"Also output power. Not as low." Roman smeared his finger across the dusty information plate to clean it. He corrected his answer, "Total output power."

Roman's mouth dried as he said the words aloud, his brain digesting their meaning faster than his body. Oliver met his gaze and nodded, but Roman didn't feel like he had won any contest.

"Total power to what?" Roman didn't need to ask. In his bones he knew. Another energy beam crashed outside. The broken door rattled against the frame. Perhaps he asked so Oliver could tell him he was wrong. But Roman knew he wasn't wrong. He also knew better than to hope that anyone else would protect him. "Are the gravity stations failing?"

Oliver didn't answer, but that was all the answer Roman needed.

"Is Icaria falling?" he asked.

"President Hinge is expecting me back tomorrow morning with someone who can help." Oliver still didn't answer the question. "Your gravity bot is your ticket in, Roman."

"Ticket into what, Oliver?" Where Oliver had used Roman's name with convincing encouragement, Roman wielded Oliver's like a weapon.

"To Icaria, *filos*." Oliver draped his arm around Roman's neck and tugged him close. Roman felt like he'd been punched in the gut. The kind touch was nothing compared to Oliver's compliment. "I know you hate the city, but I think you'll change your mind once you're up there."

Roman pulled away from Oliver. He needed space, but the room was too small. Oliver felt too close. Roman stomped to the far side of the station, breathing in the stinking air to calm his mind. Hanging on the back wall were two rubber suits with dome-like helmets. He watched his and Oliver's reflections elongate and distort in the black glass. He hadn't been called *filos* in a long time. Roman hadn't gotten close enough to anyone to be considered a brother.

"Your president said he wanted people to enroll in school. I haven't been to one in a long time." The Slums had one schoolhouse. Roman used to go with Oliver just to stay by his side, but once he was gone, Roman hadn't gone back. He'd gotten the education he needed on his own.

Oliver's reflection slowly cocked his head as a confused look claimed his face. It vanished before Roman understood what it meant. It could have been a trick of the glass. Even Roman looked different in the helmet's reflection.

Oliver nodded. "Right. I said President Hinge wanted to elevate people and cultivate their skills at the university, but Roman, you don't need to go. Not unless you want to. You're cultivated enough."

Roman eyed Oliver's hands where he tucked them under his arms, hidden from view. "You just want my sphere."

"I need you, Ro. Icaria does too."

Roman laughed at the absurdity. "You think Hinge is going to listen to what I have to say?"

Oliver shrugged. "You help me fix this, and I'm pretty sure President Hinge will give you whatever you want."

Roman gave a wicked grin, then tossed it aside. He was too close to the trap. He asked Oliver's mirrored reflection, "What makes you so sure I can help with your secret problem? Or am I the first person you found that meets the shopping list?"

"How many times do I need to say it, Ro? You're slanting brilliant."

Roman held back the snarl rising in his throat. He shook off Oliver's praise. They had both thought each other brilliant as boys, but Icaria only chose one of them.

"If the Golden Boy doesn't get home in time, I'm sure more sunkissers will come here looking for him," Roman finally answered. "I can barely stand one of you, so better get you back to your carriage before that happens."

"Roman . . ." Oliver shook his head. "Please come back with me. We need you."

Roman whirled around, his hands tightening into fists on instinct. "No. Icaria wants to use the Slums to solve their problem. You pretending that nothing's changed between us, acting like we're best friends again, saying things like I'm finally smart enough to go with you ain't going to work on me. Icaria lost their chance. I'll never help them."

Roman shoved past Oliver, yanking the door away from the frame. Dozens of blue arcs skirted across the landscape, leaving charred earth below. Sparks of energy fell from the sky. It burned the back of Roman's mouth and made every one of his hairs stand on end. He stepped outside and when his foot touched the ground, a painful current shocked him, blasting him backward.

He crashed into a broken chair, biting his tongue as his jaw clenched.

"Roman!" Oliver kneeled beside him and cupped his face with a hand. "Roman, are you okay?"

Roman swatted Oliver's hand away and spat a mouthful of blood on the ground. "Get off me."

He pushed to his feet and glared at the worsening landscape outside. The taunting feeling returned. Roman felt like a captive. Held at bay because of a little bad weather.

"The energy flux should pass," Oliver said softly behind him. "We've been tracking them for the last few months. We'll just need to wait out the storm."

Roman would have done just about anything rather than stay in the room with the sunkisser, but the leftover current running up his bones kept him in place. Just wiggling his fingers made his entire arm tense and spasm. Walking out of the station would be a death sentence. "How long?"

"Couple of hours, usually."

Biting his cheek through the pain, Roman slid the door into place and sat on the ground. He leaned his head against the cold wall, waiting for his body to stop shaking. Oliver tried and failed to start several sentences but opted to examine the gauges again. Once his hands no longer quaked, Roman tapped on his Pada to message Scrap. His message came back immediately with *failure to send no service* stamped across it.

Roman cursed again. Slanting great.

Chapter Six

Roman had slept in worse places.

The gravity station's floor was cold and hard, but it wasn't wet. The lack of food and trash made it a rat-free space, and after a while he grew used to the musky order. He balled up his jacket to use as a pillow and managed to pass some of the time with his eyes shut. Oliver's constant movement ensured he never truly went under, though. Every twenty minutes or so Oliver shifted positions. His white clothing, now gray and dingy, rustled with each movement, followed by a grunt or sigh. If they were still kids, perhaps Roman would offer him some comfort. Perhaps if Oliver hadn't left the Slums he would remember how to sleep on the ground. Perhaps Roman should have chanced walking through the energy storm.

After a few hours, Roman snapped his eyes open and glared across the room at Oliver.

"Will you cut that out?" Roman's snarl ricocheted off the walls.

"Sorry," Oliver replied, becoming still as a board. "I didn't know you were still awake."

"How can I not be with you thrashing around like that?"

Oliver sat up and stretched his arms above his head, and twisting at his waist. Some part of him popped, and he stopped. "How long has it been?"

"Don't you have a Pada?" Roman tucked his hands beneath his head, interlocking his fingers for better support. He stared at the ceiling where exposed wires had scored dark burns against the concrete structure. It was shoddy work. Probably done by a sunkisser desperate to finish the job and get back home to their comfortable beds. Roman ground his molars together.

"It's running low on battery," Oliver admitted about his Pada, sounding embarrassed.

Roman grumbled something incoherent and checked the time. Time he was running out of if he was going to report to Scrap before the gear head sold his entire establishment. He tried sending another message but, just like the four others before, it came back with *failure to send*.

"Thought you said this would only last a few hours?"

"That's the average time," Oliver answered. "But this storm seems . . . worse somehow. I guess being this close to it. It must dissipate, fizzle out, when it reaches the city."

"How long have the storms been happening?" Roman tried to remember if he'd noticed the beams shuttering before, but he couldn't be sure. Unless it helped him get his next victory, he didn't pay attention to much.

"I've been tracking them for a couple of months now," answered Oliver.

"Just you?"

Oliver smiled, satisfaction covering his grin like the dirt did his coat. "I first noticed the change in readings and brought it up to my boss. She assigned me to help the team the next day."

"They part of that patch?"

Oliver glanced down to the logo on his jacket. "Yeah. I work at Icaria Tower in the science department."

Roman chuckled. "You got a whole bunch of sunkissing scientists and can't solve this yourself?"

"I told you, Ro, we need you." Oliver's satisfied smile returned.

It made Roman uncomfortable. It made him feel like he was a prized robot in the Ring, something to be claimed. The gravity station suddenly became too small. He stood and looked outside the door's viewing window. Two blue arcs dug into the ground, ripping up gravel in their wake, but it was as calm as he'd seen it since the energy flux started. He put a newly healed knuckle to his mouth and worked the scab, thinking. This could be his best chance to escape. He couldn't chance waiting it out in case the storm kicked up again. He could dodge these slower beams easier than the sporadic jolts from earlier.

"Is this flux thing causing the power shortage?" Roman asked, stalking to the far side of the room and going through the few things left by the original operators.

"It's a result of it," Oliver answered behind him. "What are you looking for?"

Roman tossed a plastic crate of wire cutters, tubing, and other parts he didn't need away from him. "A way out of here."

"Once all this passes, we can walk right out."

Roman growled. "I don't have time to wait. Is your Pada able to send messages?"

Oliver paused before answering. "No service. Did you want to call for help?"

Roman laughed bitterly. There was no help in the Slums. If you couldn't help yourself, then you weren't fit to survive. After his search came up useless, Roman examined the two suits hanging on the back wall. Besides a few tears in the seams, the rubber material was secure. The suits were stored here for a reason; Roman bet they were left as a precaution.

He tossed his hand over his shoulder, pointing at the crate he'd slung toward Oliver. "Tape."

"What?"

"Hand me the tape," Roman said slowly. "From inside the crate."

Oliver fumbled behind him and then dropped the tape into Roman's outstretched hand. "What are you doing?"

Roman ripped a piece of the electrical tape free with his teeth and started patching one of the holes in the suit. "Leaving."

Oliver's reflection in the helmet flinched. "But the storm?"

Roman flicked the suit's helmet. "We'll use these. Icaria probably kept them as a safeguard."

"A safeguard against what?" Oliver's voice climbed higher. "I doubt these storms occurred when there were workers down here."

"You don't have to come." Roman kept his gaze on his work. It was easier to patch the holes in the suit than to repair a relationship. "You can stay here until it's safe enough for a sunkisser."

Without his Pada to use as a map, Roman doubted Oliver would find his way back to the Ring, let alone be safe about it. When the sunkissers came to the Slums to watch the robot fights, they moved in packs. It was harder for a desperate slummer to jump a bunch of them that way. If someone found Oliver wandering the Slums on his own, the energy storm would be the safer place to be.

"Is there enough tape for both?" Oliver asked before Roman could decide how he felt about these realizations.

"Should be." Roman ripped off another strip with his teeth and sealed the final rip on the first suit. He started on the second.

Oliver moved closer and peered over Roman's shoulder to observe the work. His body blocked the little light from outside and made it impossible for Roman to see the tears in the suit. Worse than the loss of vision was Oliver's scrutinizing gaze. Did Oliver see a tear that he'd missed? Did Oliver think his sunkissing hands could do it better? Was Oliver going to steal a suit and run? Roman reached behind him and shoved Oliver, and his doubts, out of the way. The contact was harsher than he intended, and Oliver collided with the broken chair and dropped to a knee. Roman didn't look at him, his hands busy with the work he knew he was doing correctly.

"Why are you so angry?" Oliver asked in a quiet voice.

Roman stared down his reflection in the helmet. He was angry about a lot of things, most of them because of the Flints, but one thing soaked his tongue in bile more than the rest. Sunkissers came down all the time to watch the fights. They were never prohibited from coming down like the slummers were from elevating.

"Why'd it take you this long to come back?" Roman ripped more of the tape to cover the crack in his voice. His throat burned as if he just drank a cup of acid rain.

Oliver ran a hand through his hair. "It's . . . it's a lot, Roman. If I could have, I would have come sooner."

Roman responded by ripping more tape. They were both silent as he finished the suits, dropping the empty roll of tape to the ground, signaling he was done. He yanked one suit off the wall and stalked to the other side of the room to step into it. It reminded him of a space suit. The puffy pants and jackets the astronauts wore before taking off in their rockets. His grandmother had seen the last rocket go up and up and up, piercing the ash clouds, until it tumbled back to earth in a blazing heap of scrap metal.

The first acid rain showers started shortly after that.

Roman zipped up his suit, pulled on the boots, and plopped his helmet down, the two ends snapping together and sealing him inside. He looked at Oliver, already in his suit, but staring down at the helmet in his hands. The oversized gloves dwarfed the reflective visor.

"I was just thinking," Oliver started, his joyful tone returning as if it could wipe away his earlier statements, "of that story you used to tell us. The one about the rocket. Do you remember?"

"No." Roman lied. The stories his grandma had passed down were for him and his best friend to retell and laugh about, not for Oliver to use against him. When Oliver left the Slums, he left all of them behind with Roman.

"Each time you told it, you changed the ending," Oliver continued. "Sometimes it was an asteroid that crashed into the rocket, other times space monsters. Liza's favorite was when the ship was sucked away in a wormhole to another world."

Roman saw it clearly in his mind. The memory populated his vision like an unwanted strike to the nose; both made his eyes water. The three of them had started a fire in one of the dumps burning strips of paper until the embers floated from their hands and disappeared into the dark sky above.

Liza had asked him to tell the story again.

"I don't think I remember it anymore," Roman had joked.

Oliver had called him a liar, matching the verbal jab with a small push at Roman's shoulder.

Roman remembered laughing, but in his mind, he didn't recognize the sound from his memory. He sounded too happy, too unaware, too content compared to the person he was now.

He'd given in to Liza like he always did. *"So, the rocket was equipped with a big lasso that the astronauts were going to use to pull the sun closer and melt the ash clouds away . . ."*

"I'm leaving," Roman declared, shaking his head free of the memory before it sucked him in further.

Oliver pulled on his helmet and followed.

Roman slid open the door and stepped outside, not giving himself time to second-guess his first step. To his relief, no electricity jolted him back. He felt a soft hum along his skin, but the suit was working. He stepped farther away from the station and craned his neck to better see the two energy arcs twisting together like a waterspout. Blue sparks fell around him and sizzled against the suit but dissipated before they caused any harm. Roman grinned, his brain rolling over different ideas he had for the suit. He was sure it would give him some edge in a future fight.

He trudged over the gravel lot, carefully avoiding the ruts caused by the energy flux. Besides the lines carved into the ground, there were several craters between the station and the hole in the fence. When Roman finally made it across the treacherous landscape, he made it alone. He turned and found Oliver standing in the middle of the lot, staring up at the floating bodies.

He wasn't watching the blue arc tumbling toward him, tearing through the ground as it approached.

"Oliver!" Roman shouted, running toward him. The thick boots made moving difficult. It felt like running through sludge. "O! Watch out!"

The beam was faster than either of them. Before Oliver could fully look at Roman, the gravity beam passed over him and sucked him into the air, his body stiff and limbs dangling. Roman ran faster, but his brain couldn't catch up with a plan. He was powerless against a three-hundred-foot gravitational beam.

He was powerless as it took his friend away.

Roman slid to a stop outside the arc's range. Every strand of his hair stood up as it tried to join the beam. He felt the pull on his insides too; his stomach was crawling up his throat. Roman grabbed a fistful of gravel and chucked it toward the beam. It had no effect, but Roman tried again. He wished he had the lasso from his story.

Oliver's body stopped rising and Roman paused in his catapulting of stones. The blue energy arc sputtered as if the faucet it came out of had turned off, and Oliver floated back to the ground slowly as the beam faded away. When it vanished completely, Oliver fell the last five feet to the ground. Roman ran to him, ripping off his helmet.

Oliver's eyes were shut, and blood trickled out of his nose. Roman placed his gloved hands on either side of Oliver's head and shook.

"O, wake up. Oliver, wake up!" Roman pulled back his hand, ready to slap him awake, but Oliver blinked his eyes open and gasped. Roman's gulps for air filled the charged silence between them.

"You good?" Roman helped Oliver sit up.

Oliver dabbed a finger under his nose and looked at the scarlet substance against the white suit glove. "What happened?"

"The beam snatched you." Roman stepped away, anger replacing the panic that had surged through him a moment ago. "What were you thinking? Standing out in the open like that? Idiot. Slanting idiot."

"I was . . ." Oliver shook his head. "Doesn't matter. Let's go before it fires up again."

Oliver struggled to get to his feet, and Roman didn't offer him any help. They passed through the fence and out of the gravity station.

Although night had changed to morning in the Slums, the darkness remained. The black barrier around the edge of the circular city had shifted to gray. The neon underside of Icaria was the ever-present oppressive sky above. Green and red circuit lights raced along the chrome. From the distance, the lights resembled stars. Or at least what Roman thought stars might look like. Neon lit the way through the dilapidated buildings and trash piles. The Slums was so quiet in this first hour of the day.

It was so quiet Roman heard the thoughts he banished. He also heard Oliver stumbling behind him to keep up in the clunky suit.

With the helmet's visor pushed back, Roman used his mouth to yank off his gloves and accessed his Pada.

"Slants," he cursed.

"What happened?" Oliver asked, waddling beside him.

"Nothing." Roman lowered his arm. The light from the Pada vanished inside his sleeve. He was two hours past his time limit.

Oliver swallowed. "Before I leave, can I charge my Pada at your place?"

"If it's still mine."

"What's that mean?"

"Nothing." Roman gritted his teeth. "What's going to happen when you go back empty-handed?"

"Are you asking because you care?"

"No." Roman's answer was as short as a fried circuit.

Oliver shrugged, but even the helmet couldn't hide the smile creeping along his face. "I think you're lying."

"Why would I care about a city full of sunkissers?"

"I don't doubt that, but I think you care about me. Why else would you try and save me from the beam?"

Roman paused for half a heartbeat, then continued walking.

"I saw you when I was in the beam." Oliver's know-it-all tone was aggravating. "Were you throwing rocks?"

"You didn't see shit." Roman tried to slide his hands inside his pockets but couldn't through his suit. His hands fisted at his sides.

Oliver chuckled. "So, my Pada?"

"Yeah, sure. Whatever."

Dead Dove wasn't in flames when Roman approached, which settled his nerves slightly. The bar was just as he left it last night, nothing stolen or sold in his absence. Even Scrap still sat at the bar, his head resting atop his arms. His soft snoring filled the empty space. Roman slammed the door shut behind them, and Scrap shot up. A strand of drool linked his chin to the bar top.

"Ro!" Scrap greeted loudly. "You came back."

"Didn't think I would?" Roman asked.

"Well, no, I mean, you didn't message but—"

"But," Roman interrupted, "my place is still here."

Scrap blushed. "You really think I'd follow through right at twelve hours?"

"You should follow through on all your deals," Roman said. "You would've been rich this morning if you had."

"Nah man, I'm better off with you in charge."

Roman grinned, throwing himself into one of the bar stools beside Scrap. The gear-head wouldn't know the first thing about running a club like Dead Dove, and the parts in the workshop wouldn't last him forever. Scrap was right. He was better off with Roman calling the shots. Still, Roman thought, placing a knuckle against his teeth, selling Dead Dove would have made Scrap's next couple of years easy. Easy to get food, easy to get drink, easy to feel safe inside a prep room with more advanced locks.

Scrap settled back in his seat and rubbed the connections where his metal arm attached to the remaining skin on his forearm. The chrome joints at the elbow and wrist were tarnishing and, when Scrap moved, they whined like a dying rat. Roman pulled his knuckle out of his mouth when Scrap caught him staring.

"Dove looks good," Roman said. It was the closest thing Roman could give to a compliment.

"Cleaned it like I do every night," Scrap replied with a proud beam. "Tansy's on her way over too. Didn't know when you'd be back, so I slept here in case she needed to be let in."

It wasn't the first time Roman found Scrap sleeping in his bar. Decent homes were hard to find and harder to afford in the Slums. Ever since the infection took his arm as a boy, Scrap had been cast out of his bed for fear of spreading something. Even his family didn't want him back. Roman was certain they couldn't look at him after leaving him at a clinic when his arm was amputated. They couldn't afford the operation or the compassion.

Roman stood and moved toward the back door to his workshop to grab his tools. "I'll tune up your arm."

"Thanks, Ro." Scrap sounded shocked but didn't question Roman's sudden generosity. "I could really use it."

"My Pada?" Oliver awkwardly voiced behind them. He stuck out like a broken finger wearing the rubber suit and helmet inside Dead Dove, but he still looked less out-of-place than in the Icarian clothes he wore yesterday.

"That the sunkisser?" Scrap asked Roman, finally noticing their matching suits. "What kind of errand were you on?"

"A boring one," Roman answered, then he addressed Oliver. "Charging station is at that booth. Two cryptens for every five percent. Twenty percent minimum."

"You're charging me?" Oliver asked.

"Nothing's free in the Slums," Scrap answered before Roman could.

Oliver retired to the booth. Roman watched Oliver struggle to fit a cable that was more duct tape than cord into his tiny Pada, then he entered his workshop. His shop was the cleanest space in Dead Dove. The long shipping container room was lit by clear neon tubing running across the ceiling. The tables—some made of metal sheets and some of old doors—were organized by stages of projects: some piles of material and some finished bots. His gravity sphere sat in the middle of the room atop a steel-legged table.

Roman ran specs on his machine to make sure it hadn't been tampered with since he last used it at the fight. The readings came back clear. His sphere was as perfect as he left it. The tiny robot was still capable of destroying so many sunkisser bots in a matter of minutes. His mind shifted to the blue energy beam at the gravity station. If he could incorporate that kind of output into his bot, he'd be unstoppable. His bot could only absorb a small percentage of power and turn it into an electromagnet, but if he could find a way for the bot to create its own gravity . . .

Or if Roman could harness the gravity beam at the station . . .

Roman slid out of the rubber suit and set it and the helmet on the table next to his sphere. Once Oliver was gone, he'd be able to focus on his build. Roman grabbed his tools and rejoined Scrap at the bar.

"You look better." Scrap laid his arm across the bar top as Roman sat back down. "Black's a better color on you."

Roman opened his toolbox, snapped on a pair of black goggles, and sparked to life a tiny welding torch. Its green flame was too bright to look at head-on, and Scrap turned away.

"Just not used to seeing you in white is all. You came back looking like a . . . ouch!"

Roman moved the welding flame away from Scrap's skin. "What's the arm been doing?"

"Locking up at the fingers," Scrap answered, dropping his observation about Roman's appearance.

Roman worked the joints of the arm. As he pulled back the outer casing, he saw the numerous upgrades he'd done to the prosthetic. The layers becoming a catalog of all his improvements. The chrome fell away to steel, to iron, to brass, to aluminum. Scrap's arm was a living time capsule of all Roman had learned. Scrap had been just a boy, barely younger than Roman, when he agreed to let Roman attach the handmade arm. The pain of his missing limb had probably made Scrap delirious. No one in their right mind would have let a grease covered fourteen-year-old Roman play doctor.

"Better already." Scrap flexed his fingers when Roman pulled the torch away.

"Hold still." Roman replaced his welder with a screwdriver and set to work tightening the connections. "Have you been using the oil like I showed you?"

"Every day," Scrap said. "Well, every day that I can find the stuff."

Roman shook his head. "Use that scratch I pay you to buy some. You won't need as much maintenance if you do."

"Thanks, Roman."

"I ain't doing it for you," Roman snapped. "I'm worried about my arm, is all. It's good work. It should be treated better."

"Yeah, yeah." Scrap chuckled, then asked in a lower voice, "So, what's up with the sunkisser? Where'd you go last night? You aren't wearing my tech, so I was actually worried about you, ya know?"

"Icaria's just trying to get me to buy something."

"How's the deal?"

"Deadly. Won't give me all the details."

"What do you know?"

Roman knew next to nothing. He knew the gravity stations were losing power, and he knew if Icaria stopped floating, then the only place it would crash would be on top of the Slums. Roman knew if the Slums survived the impact, they wouldn't survive the acid rain. Roman didn't know what he was supposed to do.

He wouldn't be a king without a ring to fight in.

He wouldn't be himself if he helped the sunkissers. They deserved to fall.

He would be an absolute fool to trust Oliver again.

"Ro, ouch, Roman, that's good." Scrap yanked his arm away from Roman and his screwdriver before it could strip away the screw.

He could become the king to all of the Slums if he brought Icaria advancements back with him. If he controlled clean water, real food, actual medicine, he would control the entire world. He could own a hundred Dead Doves. He could have the nicest prep room. Hell, he could own the entire slanting Ring.

Roman shoved his barstool back and pointed his screwdriver at Oliver. A toxic mixture of hope and fear painted Oliver's face. The charging wire tethered him to the wall, making him look like a trapped rabbit. Roman grinned like the fox he was.

"Say I go up with you," Roman said, "I'll need some assurances that me and my stuff will be taken care of."

"Up where?" Scrap asked.

"Whatever you need," Oliver promised.

"Scrap," Roman turned to his mechanic. "You'll need to run Dead Dove for me."

"Run the Dove? Roman, what's going on?"

"I'm going to Icaria," Roman answered Scrap, then turned to Oliver. "I'll fix their little gravity problem."

He wasn't sure how, but Roman doubted it would be impossible. He was slanting brilliant after all.

"You will?" Oliver's face shone with delight. He stepped away from the booth, tearing himself free of the cable.

"Yeah, but I'll come back whenever I want to."

"Of course, Icaria isn't a . . ." Oliver changed topic. "Let's get going. The sooner we're there the better."

"I'm grabbing a few things first." Roman tossed his screwdriver in his toolbox and carried it toward the door marked with his four-pointed crown.

"Ro, wait!" Scrap slid off his chair and followed him. "Are you out of your slanting mind? What is happening? Who is that guy?"

"I got hired for a job," Roman answered flatly, walking into his workshop. "This room is off-limits while I'm gone. Everything you need for the Dove is in the office, got it?"

"Course, Ro, but come on. A job in Icaria? Don't they have everything they need up there?"

Roman sneered. "They ain't got me."

"Sure, but Roman . . ." Scrap picked up a wrench and ran his thumb over the tuner.

"Cut it, Scrap." Roman stopped fitting his sphere into a crate to look at him. "Say what you're thinking."

Scrap blushed and blurted out, "Are you going to come back? When the job's over and they pay you, will you come back?"

Roman laughed. "That's the best thing, Scrap. They're going to pay me with the city. Once I solve their little problem, I'm taking the city for us. All the stuff that makes that city so great I'm bringing it down here. We're going to be kings."

"You mean it?" Scrap's eyes lit up like the welding torch.

Roman nodded and continued packing. He hadn't intended to include Scrap in his monarchy. It was a slip of the tongue in his excitement. Roman wasn't going to share his future empire, but he would make sure Scrap had some place to lay his head that wasn't behind a dumpster or a bar top. His mechanic was worth that much.

"What if they don't like that? The sunkissers?"

Roman grabbed the wrench from Scrap and pointed it at him. "Any sunkisser that has a problem with me can think it over down here. I'm taking over, Scrap. You got it?"

Scrap straightened his back and offered a small salute. "Got it, boss."

Chapter Seven

After cramming a few extra clothes and his favorite tools into a backpack, Roman entered his office to scribble down a to-do list for Scrap. Roman didn't expect to be gone for too long, but there would be a stardust shipment to pay for and the beer tap needed reconfiguration before it started leaking again. Roman knew Scrap could keep basic inventory and his mechanical know-how would cover the tap, and Tansy would handle the hospitality of the bar, but a concrete list wouldn't hurt. He tucked the crate containing his sphere under his arm and reentered the main room of Dead Dove. Scrap sat with his back to the bar, keeping a hawk-like watch on Oliver seated at the charging booth, his space suit folded politely on the table.

Roman watched their silent interactions from the doorway. He was partly amused at how the situation made Oliver look uncomfortable and partly proud of Scrap for taking on this task on his own. Oliver attempted to keep his eyes on anything other than Scrap, but Roman didn't miss his gaze drifting to Tansy, who leaned against the bar. Scrap made some kind of gesture that Roman couldn't see, and Oliver dropped his eyes, his fingers tapping against the table.

Roman set his to-do list on the bar and tapped it until Scrap changed his focus to him.

Scrap laughed under his breath after he finished reading the list. "I'm surprised you didn't add 'no free drinks' on here."

"You better not need that reminder," Roman said. "Or you, Tansy."

Tansy scoffed at the idea. "This list makes me feel like you don't trust us at all. There's even instructions to the deep fryer. How long have I worked here, Ro?"

Probably too long, but Roman didn't answer her. He looked at Oliver and said, "Come here."

Oliver unplugged his Pada and joined them at the bar. He didn't look any more relaxed being beside Roman. Oliver kept his limbs pressed tightly to his sides to not take up any more room than necessary. "Yeah?"

"Write your contact on here."

Both Scrap and Oliver blinked at Roman as if he'd spoken in a dead language.

Roman clarified, "In case my Pada doesn't connect way up there, I need a way for Scrap to get a hold of me."

Oliver accepted his reason and scribbled a series of numbers on the top of the page.

"When the dust delivery comes in," Roman told Scrap, "I'll wire you the scratch so you can pay it."

"You should pay him now," Tansy said, then added when Roman's stare tried to vaporize her, "In case you don't have a connection in Icaria. Bruno's not a patient man, you know this."

"I wouldn't give that dust-head a single crypten early even if my life depended on it," Roman barked.

"Just our lives?" Tansy crossed her arms. "Those runners are monsters, right Scrap?"

Scrap didn't back her up, but he didn't deny it. Dust runners were more beast than man, Bruno and his gang in particular. Their rage and greed were fueled by inhaling the fumes of distilling stardust. Roman hated doing business with Bruno, but at least he knew the dust was clean, and Dead Dove's customers lined up for it too. Some of the less respectable distillers cut their liquor with acid rain. The liquor coated the acid for a short span which made drinking it safe for the mouth but lethal in the gut.

Before Roman could respond and probably make the situation worse, Oliver smoothed things over with his educated voice.

"If Ro doesn't have service, I'll make sure you get the payment," he told Tansy. "I'll wire you the cryptens right now if you want."

She smiled, but her words were not as friendly. "I'm surprised Ro hasn't taught you yet. You don't ever lend out your scratch. You won't get it back."

Oliver blushed. "I didn't realize that."

Scrap leaned into Tansy and said, "The kisser's not one of us. He's just a job."

"Speaking of which," Roman interrupted, "did the sunkisser pay his charging fee?"

"Yep," Scrap answered. "One hundred percent."

"I'm still thirty percent short." Oliver checked his Pada for confirmation.

"That'll be enough to get you home," Roman said to him. "Dead Dove thanks you for your tip."

Ignoring his comment, Oliver eyed the crate. "Is that it? Your gravity bot?"

"Yeah," Roman snapped. "You got a problem with me bringing it?"

"No, no." Oliver held up his hands. "I just thought it'd be bigger is all."

"You saw the fight." Roman was still defensive, looking for any flaw in Oliver. "Unless you lied."

"I saw your fight," Oliver said slowly, stating each word so Roman had no excuse but to hear him. "All the bots looked small from my seat."

Roman eyed Oliver, deciding if he believed him. The Ring had several box seats at the top where the wealthiest sunkissers could purchase tickets. The joke among the slummers was those kissers were scared to be too far from Icaria so the box seats were the closest they could be to home without sitting on the roof. The way Oliver shifted about the Slums, always ready to bolt out a door, Roman could believe the joke.

The laboratory logo stitched on his coat's breast pocket made Roman believe Oliver could afford the ticket too.

Roman turned to Scrap. "Don't let anyone know I'm gone."

"What should I say if they ask?"

"Make something up." Roman shrugged. "Tell them I'm holed up in the workshop or something. Tansy can drop off food there if anyone gets suspicious. Yeah, you can eat it after shift."

Scrap smiled, tucking the to-do list into his back pocket. "You should go on business trips more often. This is going to be great."

"Whatever," Roman said. "Don't let Dead Dove burn."

"It was nice to meet you," Oliver said to them, but only looked at Tansy. "I think your star tattoos look nice."

Roman shoved Oliver toward the door before Scrap could react.

As they approached Oliver's carriage around the block, two slummers scurried out from under it. Roman recognized the tiny welding torch in their hands. It was the same kind he used on Scrap. The flame was small, but it could rip into metal without much fuss. A charred scent wafted through the air. If anything was left on the underside of the carriage, it was probably an ashy and useless mess. Roman regretted not drawing his crown on the carriage the night before. He gritted his teeth.

"Don't worry about them," Oliver said.

"Your ride's ruined."

"Not my model." Oliver tapped his Pada watch against the side of the carriage. "Nothing short of a Byzing blowtorch will melt the outside casing."

A low whistle escaped Roman, but he refused to let his jaw drop. A slummer could only dream of accessing a level of disruptive power like a Byzing blowtorch. The flame it produced was rumored to be seen from space. It could slice open a diamond like paper.

A keypad flipped out of the carriage where Oliver tapped his Pada, and he typed in an entry key. Artificially-scented air tumbled out as the door slid open. Roman followed Oliver inside and tossed himself against one of the two plush bench seats. Chrome fixings ran along the seams and around the blacked-out windows. Stamped onto the top of the domed ceiling was a curling F that probably stood for Flint.

The door shut.

"Destination?" prompted an automated voice from an overhead speaker.

"Elevation platform," Oliver replied.

After a series of beeps, the voice returned. "Destination found. Arrival time is twelve minutes. Beginning transportation."

"Pretty chatty for a robot," Roman muttered as the carriage moved forward. He looked around for the speaker, wanting to track the wiring to a control box, but the interior was free of mechanics. Roman assumed the hardware was encased between the two shells that made up the carriage. Out of sight and out of mind. It was an ugly design. He wanted to know how it operated.

"I thought you'd find the voice controls interesting."

As ridiculous as the carriage was, its size was not impressive. Roman sat a foot away from Oliver. The bench seats forced them to stare at each other. The artificial air stung the inside of his nose. He tapped his fingers against the top of his sphere.

"Pretty lame you don't have windows," he grumbled.

Oliver smirked. "Window darkness zero percent."

Quicker than a finger snap, grey light filled the carriage as the blackened windows lightened to pure glass. The Slums slipped by. People stared into the carriage, whispering among each other and hurling insults at the occupants. Roman leaned deeper into his seat, trying to avoid detection.

"Undo window darkness," Oliver said, and the black windows returned. "This is the newest model, and I'm still working out some of the details."

"You built this?" Roman raised an eyebrow.

"Programmed," Oliver corrected. "A mechanic put it together."

"Still won't get your hands dirty with the construction, will you?"

"You know I was never good at that," Oliver admitted. "At university I could focus on what I wanted, and I stuck with coding. It paid off."

It was uncomfortable to watch him brag. The ruddy-faced boy Roman had grown up with was shyer than a mouse. It was a surprise a rat hadn't eaten him while he was still in the Slums. University must have changed more about him than just his education levels. Roman scoffed. It was probably a lousy place. Roman had taught himself mechanics and coding without anything more than broken parts and robot pilots to eavesdrop on.

"What would be exciting," Oliver dragged Roman back into the present, "is if we teamed up on a project, again. Like old times."

"I ain't building your dumb cars."

"It doesn't have to be a carriage," Oliver said. "I'd like to build a bot with you."

"Just like old times." Roman gritted his teeth before setting a healing knuckle against them. The blood in his mouth offered a comforting familiarity. He was used to seeing an oncoming attack. Whether a person or a robot, most things had a tell that gave them away. Roman watched Oliver to spot his, but an attack never came. Oliver's request hung in the air.

The twelve minutes to the elevation platform felt far longer than it should have, and when they arrived Roman was happy for the peace that it brought. Oliver left the carriage to show his identification card to the enforcer, and Roman soaked in the silence with his eyes shut. After a few minutes, Oliver returned, and the carriage rose.

"Window darkness zero percent."

Roman opened his eyes, about to snap about wanting the windows off, but stopped when he looked outside. The Slums vanished below him. The ring of enforcers around the elevation platform became microscopic. The old-world buildings of the Slums turned into ants as the carriage ascended. The streets he'd lived on his entire life became part of a mess of crosshatching lines among piles of rubbish. Even the Ring looked like a marble. Roman had never realized how far Icaria truly was from them until now.

"Window darkness fifty percent."

"Hey!" Roman barked, wanting to see more of his home and, more importantly, Icaria.

"You'll thank me," Oliver assured, a smug look claiming his face. "Just hang on."

Darkness filled the carriage as it moved through the bottom of the disk. When it emerged on the other side, light exploded inside the cab. Roman shielded his eyes until they stopped burning and slowly lowered his hand to look out the window.

Icaria was immaculate.

The streets were white stone. Green plants grew in the thin space between the road and sidewalk. Pedestrians didn't gawk at the carriage like the slummers did. A chrome onion-shaped vehicle moving through a glass tunnel was a common sight for them. More carriages moved freely down the street unconfined by the track leading Oliver's carriage away from the elevation platform. The sunkissers wore clothing of seamless fabrics instead of the pieced-together textiles Roman knew. Buildings stretched high into the sky with their uniform walls and intact windows. Roman pressed his nose against the glass to better see the sky.

His grandma had told him it was blue. He thought he knew what that color was until now. This blue was water: cool and wet and refreshing. This blue was soft: simple and smooth and clean. This blue was breathless: airy, and expansive, and pure. Roman felt like he could stare at it forever. He wanted to find every secret that was hidden there.

Darkness covered the carriage.

"Put the windows back down," he ordered Oliver.

"We're inside a building," Oliver explained.

Roman squinted against the glass and noticed the concrete wall on the other side. He slumped against the bench seat. Oliver chuckled, which made Roman scowl. He was getting tired of being the butt of all of Oliver's unknown jokes.

"The carriage has to be decontaminated before we can enter the city," Oliver said. "To make sure nothing came up with us."

"You mean stowaways."

Oliver didn't answer. The carriage slowed to a stop before rattling as a gust of air blasted it from the top. A red light filled the cab while some kind of beam scanned the outside of the carriage. Roman shouldered his backpack and grabbed his crate so he'd have something to do besides being inspected by Oliver.

"Decontamination complete," the automatic voice said over the carriage's speakers. "Welcome back to Icaria, Mr. Flint and guest."

"Program mode," Oliver prompted, sounding far more formal than conversational with the voice. "Add current guest, Roman Koa, to contacts. Status: User."

The carriage beeped. "Request complete. Welcome back to Icaria, Mr. Flint, and Mr. Koa."

"Did you just give me keys to this thing?" Roman asked. He wanted to sound uncaring, but his fingers twitched with excitement at the thought of taking the carriage for himself.

"You don't have the code to open the door." Oliver grinned, opening that very door to exit the carriage. "But when you're inside, you can control the windows."

Roman rolled his eyes and followed Oliver out of the carriage.

The decontamination center was free of enforcers. Roman almost found it surprising until he remembered that no one would be trying to sneak into the Slums. Icarian enforcers and robots patrolled the elevation platform back home every hour to ensure only sunkissers made it into Icaria. Roman followed Oliver into a glass booth barely wide enough for the both of them. He didn't try to make the space comfortable; he squared his shoulders and took up as much room as he could.

"What is this place?" he asked.

"Final step in the process," Oliver answered.

Jets of scented air blasted them from above and knocked dirt from Roman's hair onto the floor. When the assault was over, a ring of dust lay around Roman's black boots.

"You smell better," Oliver said with a laugh as the glass door on the other side of the containment room slid open. "But, *filos*, you're going to need a shower before we do anything."

"Shouldn't fixing your gravity problem come first?" Roman took a whiff of himself but couldn't smell a difference. "Shouldn't we go see Hinge, or some science lab?"

"It'll be easier to concentrate without the smell, and with a full stomach. Hungry?"

Roman followed him out of the glass room at the promise of food. In the Slums he'd become so used to smelling the mixture of trash, acid rain, and motor oil that its absence was alarming. He inhaled deeply several times, but fear gripped his throat. His body believed that he wasn't ingesting any oxygen. His breathing shallowed. He tightened a fist against his heart and felt it beat. He was breathing. He was living. Without the garbage smell to shift through, Roman smelled nothing. He just felt the air entering and leaving his lungs. It was unsettling.

Oliver kept moving ahead of him without noticing Roman's panic attack. He tapped his Pada against the computer screen to the left of a double door and light filled the room as the doors separated. Roman felt the heat of the sun before the light reached him. It made the skin on his face prickle. He didn't raise his hand to shield his eyes as the white light bathed him and caused tears to well up. He embraced the light and the heat. He embraced the sizzling sensation on his skin. He embraced the heaviness of his eyes. He embraced what would be his. The sun. The clean air. The warmth. Icaria.

Roman followed Oliver outside. What he'd just embraced inside the decontamination center suffocated him now that he stood in the sunlight completely.

Every breath was a struggle as the hot air burned his lungs. The second Roman inflated his chest with air, the oppressive heat pressed it out of him. The sizzle on his bare arms turned into a burn, and his tattoos itched worse than the day he got them. He squinted against the light and shielded his face with the back of his hand. Against his will, Roman's body stepped backward toward the comfort of the darkened interior of the decontamination center.

Oliver handed something to him, and when Roman didn't accept it right away, Oliver tapped the object against Roman's hand.

"Sunglasses," Oliver called them after Roman grabbed the object. "Those will protect your eyes. You probably should wear sunblock too. Until your body is used to the rays."

Roman slipped on the glasses and was able to see again. Oliver wore a pair too, although his were slimmer and covered less of his face. The world around him was a merciful shade darker with them on. The slummers had always called those who lived in Icaria sunkissers because the people were high enough to kiss the sun. Now, standing under it, Roman realized the nickname should have been a reference to how the sun kissed them. Viciously. Angrily. Relentlessly.

Roman soaked in the heat. The sun was just like him. Eager to claim what it wanted and destroy what it didn't.

Oliver shrugged out of his white jacket and held it out to Roman. "The walk to my house might actually burn you, now that I think of it. There's sunblock at home, but until then, wear my coat."

Roman turned his nose up at the offering. He could handle the sun burn, whatever that was.

Oliver yanked the crate out of Roman's hands and thrust the coat into them. "I mean it, Ro. Wear the jacket or I'm taking you back."

Roman grumbled but stuck his arms through the sleeves. "Not worried about me getting my stink on it?"

"I'll wash it," Oliver answered, clearly relieved that Roman had put the coat on. He handed the crate back.

Roman gripped his crate tightly as Oliver looked him over, dragging his gaze from the top of his head to the soles of his boots. Roman had never wanted to hit him more. "What?"

"Nothing." Oliver met Roman's glare with a smile. "Let's go."

Roman tried to walk by Oliver's side, but he kept falling back as things grabbed his attention. Actual grass grew in orderly stripes next to the sidewalk. Under the clean air, he smelled things he couldn't name. An orange and black butterfly fluttered ahead of him. A cat lounged atop a building's front steps with a belly fuller than Roman's had ever been.

"Look different from how you imagined it?" Oliver asked, pausing for him to catch up. He looked comfortable on these streets, his hands hanging loosely at his sides. "I was surprised the buildings weren't actually gold when we got here."

"It's taller," Roman answered, looking down either side of the street. Multiple-story buildings lined both sides with businesses on the bottom floor and what Roman assumed were apartments in the upper levels, based on the furniture he saw in the windows. In the distance, a silver tower rose higher than the other buildings.

"There are gardens on the rooftops," Oliver said, pointing at the buildings on either side of the street. "To grow food."

"Must be nice." Very rarely did the sunkissers throw out produce, and very rarely did gardens in the Slums produce anything more than rhubarb and fungus under the neon lights.

"Come on," Oliver turned to his left. "I can show you more of the city later."

"Why not now?" Roman shifted the crate onto his hip and followed Oliver, mapping the streets back to the decontamination center in case he needed to get back home in a hurry.

"I wasn't kidding about the shower." Oliver playfully waved his hand in front of his nose. "Not to mention Liza will want to see you."

Roman was more prepared to stare at the sun than to see Oliver's little sister.

"I just want to fix the gravity and go." Roman didn't think Oliver needed to know the other part of his plan.

Oliver shot him a sideways glare that didn't sit well on his newly minted cheery face. Roman raised an eyebrow, waiting for his response, but all Oliver did was lead him across the street. They walked into a group of sunkissers sipping on iced drinks. One watched them cross the road, and Roman readied a snarl, but she didn't comment on him. Instead, she smiled and waved at them both before turning back to her friend's conversation.

Roman eyed the woman and then the white coat he'd been forced to wear. "You weren't worried about the burns."

"No, I wasn't." Oliver's honesty surprised Roman. "It's easier this way. For now."

"For now?" Roman echoed.

"To them, right now, you're just a slummer." Oliver's words weren't kind, but Roman wasn't looking for kindness. "They still treat me and Liza like that too, sometimes. The ones who remember."

Roman looked away from the scattering crowd. "Remember?"

"Where we came from," Oliver answered in a low voice, his hand rising to the scar under his left ear before falling to his side. "Can we not talk about that right now, or the reason you're here? It'll make people nervous."

"Whatever." Roman stepped around Oliver, who jogged ahead so he could continue to lead the way through Icaria.

Roman had known the city would differ from the Slums, but he couldn't get over the vastness of those differences. Every building stretching and stretching high above, while the tallest thing in the Slums was the Ring. The blue sky appearing in strips between their roofs. People meandering outside stores and under trees with nothing to do except stand in Roman's way. There was no down-time in the Slums. Roman spent every moment keeping himself alive. Birds chirped above him sounding too cheerful. Even they meandered because they didn't fear someone catching and eating them. The sunkissers probably had a way to grow meat.

Another secret they kept from the Slums.

Another secret that Roman would take from them.

"What's great about this place?" Roman asked, the insults soothing his mind. He lifted the sunglasses to look at a bird perched on a branch and hissed when the light and heat seared his eyes. He dropped the shades before anyone could see the water leaking from them.

Oliver gestured around them. He pointed at the sturdy buildings, the abundant plant life, the fat bird in the tree. Oliver turned and pointed at the carriages rumbling by, the pristine streets, the blue sky. Roman shrugged, swallowing down his jealousy. It was just fanfare. Homes, food, roads. He had them in the Slums, although nowhere near as nice.

"Nothing is changing my mind," Roman taunted.

"I'll show you more later." Oliver was unaffected by his prickly mood.

"Show me now," Roman demanded, blocking Oliver's path.

Oliver twisted his hands together before stowing them inside his pockets. "We really need to get home. I'll take you out later. I promise."

"I'm not some dumb dog," Roman said.

Oliver didn't respond. He stood as sturdy on the sidewalk as the buildings did beside them. Despite the expansive world around him, Roman felt it closing in. He needed to regain control. He needed to tear something apart. Roman needed to understand this strange world that stole Oliver from him, and then he needed to take it for himself.

Roman stepped off the sidewalk, narrowly missing an oncoming carriage that honked its displeasure as it drove by. He took off near the closest alleyway. Before he could cross the street, Oliver snatched his wrist and pulled him back. Roman jerked away, crouching low and ready to fight.

"Okay," Oliver surrendered. "There's something I can show you. It's along the way to my house."

"What is it?" Roman asked, refusing to follow Oliver until he knew more.

"A surprise."

Roman wanted to shake Oliver until he knocked the playful grin off his face. Instead, he gritted his teeth and stepped back onto the sidewalk.

Oliver led the way down several short streets before emerging into a small courtyard. As Roman stepped onto the grass, his boots sank into the lush texture. He kneeled to touch it and gasped. It was so soft. It was almost uncomfortably soft. Roman couldn't understand how the feathery feel both hurt and soothed him. He wiped his hands down his pants as he straightened, letting the coarseness of the fabric wash away the sensation of the grass.

A wooden structure about as tall as Roman stood in the center of the courtyard. He didn't understand what it was supposed to be. Four gnarly antlers rose from the ground on either side of it and curved outward, making an incomplete circle. Roman walked around it but, even with the new angles, couldn't decide what it was.

"This it?" he asked Oliver.

"Give me a second." Oliver powered on his Pada, the digital display expanding above his arm, and typed in a coded sequence. Once he finished, the Pada beeped, and a thin green beam of light connected it to the wooden structure. The tips of the antlers glowed green as it accepted the code and then it came to life.

Roman stepped back as hologram flowers blossomed down the structure. The blooms swirled in pink and purple light, vibrant leaves sprouted under them, and vines stretched across the antler's tops, creating a gazebo of light. A herd of deer materialized in the center and stepped onto the lush grass. Their ears flicked in response to actual noises, their hooves flattened the real grass like Roman's boots had. One approached Roman and stood a foot away. Roman felt the heat of the animal's breath. He saw himself reflected in its eyes.

The show of technology was impressive, but Roman had seen it before. In a cruder, younger state. Originally, it had materialized rats running through trash piles in the Slums. Those hologram constructs had flickered more than these deer did. Roman had never believed he could actually feel the rat's fur like he thought he could if he reached out and touched the deer now. It disgusted him.

"This is your code," he accused.

Oliver flinched. The deer closest to him flinched as well.

"Icaria took you for this code and you used it to make slanting deer?" Roman marched toward Oliver and the deer bolted back to the safety of the wooden structure. "You left for this?"

"This isn't the only thing it's used for!" Oliver shouted back. "You liked it when I made rats and bugs. I thought you'd like seeing this."

Roman had liked watching Oliver make the holograms. He had liked seeing Oliver write code in the dirt before programming it into the old microwave Roman had salvaged for hardware. He had liked using the bugs to scare Liza. He had liked falling down into a laughing fit with Oliver when their trick worked, and Liza swatted at them. He had liked Oliver being in the Slums with him.

Not the slanting *animals*.

"I'm sorry it's not being used for robot fights," Oliver was saying when Roman disentangled himself from his memories. "We're using it to preserve parts of the Earth that were lost after the eruptions."

Roman took a heavy breath. Oliver and Icaria were using the code now. Icaria was using Oliver now. This was what Oliver chose over him. This shiny and sturdy world where people could spend their time watching deer in a park and not worry if they would eat that day.

Roman needed this city.

"Where's your house?" he asked.

Oliver sighed and deactivated his hologram. The deer melted down to ones and zeroes while the flowers withered and vanished. It was very theatrical. It was very Oliver Flint.

Oliver led on through more streets that all looked the same except for the awning colors above businesses before turning down a final street marked with lamp posts. The same building lined the entire street like they'd been mass-produced by some factory. Five concrete steps led to a wooden door with white columns on either side. Four mail slots marked with apartment numbers were built into the right side of the door. As he had with the carriage, Oliver held his Pada against a scanner and a keypad folded down from the wall. He entered a code.

"Home sweet home," Oliver said as the door opened, revealing a wide hallway ending in a grand staircase.

Roman stepped inside and noticed four doors with numbers that matched the mail slots. Two were on this level and two more were at the top of the stairs.

"We're number three." Oliver shut the door, and a series of clicks set the lock back in place.

"Do I get guest access here too?" Roman asked, following Oliver up the stairs to the door on the left.

"It won't be necessary," Oliver answered, using his Pada to unlock the apartment door. "I'll be with you whenever you need to leave."

"You make this sound like a prison."

"Then it's the nicest prison in the world." Oliver pushed open the door and ushered Roman inside.

This was not an apartment. This was a throne room. This was a display of wealth and excellence for the simple pleasure of being able to display it. Soft sunlight cascaded across the tiled floor through windows overlooking Icaria. Sparkling chandeliers hung from the high ceiling. White furniture adorned with gold and green accents populated sections of the open room in designated eating, sitting, and reading atmospheres. A kitchen creeped out of the back corner with long counters and deep cabinets, silver appliances glistening in the sunlight. Another staircase twisted up opposite the kitchen leading to a balcony where more doors led to probably more extravagant rooms.

Roman turned in circles, trying to take in everything, but at each turn he discovered something new. A small ceramic elephant atop a dresser. A bookshelf filled with more books than he knew existed. A painting of the four Flints hanging on the wall. A robot fighter in the corner now being used as a coat hanger.

"There's a room for you upstairs," Oliver said, waiting for him at the bottom of the staircase. "Get cleaned up and I'll make some lunch."

Roman huffed. "Extra beds. Extra food. I can see why you didn't come back."

"Just come on," Oliver said, discomfort crossing his cheerful face for a moment.

Roman followed him upstairs to a bedroom the size of Dead Dove. It didn't just have an extra bed; the room was furnished with enough stuff that if he sold it in the Slums he'd easily make a fortune. He could see his new title: Roman Koa, Furniture King. He set his crate on the desk and turned to Oliver. This would be the time to say thank you, but Roman didn't know how. He wasn't sure if he was thankful.

"Bathroom's there," Oliver pointed to one of the doors, "and there's clean clothes in the closet. They'll have to do until we get you your own."

"What's wrong with mine?"

"Besides the oil stains and the smell, they're too . . . They don't . . ."

"Say it, Oliver."

"They don't look right," he said with a polite smile.

Roman heard what Oliver actually meant. They didn't belong here. Like Roman. He slid out of Oliver's coat and threw it at him.

"You want me to blend in." Roman crossed his arms, his grime and tattoos and bloody knuckles on display. "Too embarrassed to have a slummer as a roommate? A slummer you brought up here to solve your problem?"

Oliver's smile did not waver. "There's nothing I could dress you up in to make you blend in. You're too . . . You're too you."

This time his words did sound like a good thing, but Roman didn't accept them. They were sweet and sticky and the perfect bait for a trap.

"Shower," Oliver prompted, stepping back into the hallway and closing the door.

Chapter Eight

Dirty water kept dripping off Roman despite his efforts to clean himself. His arms and legs were raw from the numerous times he ran the soapy washcloth over them. His fingernails came back with dirt under them every time he rinsed his hair. The steamy enclosure of the bathroom smelled nice, so at least Roman would smell better even if he couldn't remove all of the dirt. He shut off the water and watched the last drops roll off him.

Showering with pure water was a luxury he would not soon forget. The way his eyes burned from the soap was something he hoped wouldn't last, though. He yanked a towel off the rack and dried himself off, rubbing the material over his head until his black hair became a tangled mess. He tossed the towel in the tub when he was done.

The Roman standing in the mirror still looked like him. The same green snake tattoo ran up his wrist to his forearm. Inky swirls manifested on his other arm in chaotic waves. The charms against his ribs depicted a sparrow, an exploding rocket, and a mechanical fist. Their colors had been brought to life by the shower. Roman poked at the rocket tattoo. His finger dipped between two ribs. All three charms fell in between the bones of his chest. He was a walking skeleton.

Wet footprints soaked into the bedroom carpet as he stalked over to the closet. Roman rolled his eyes at the contents. Everything inside was brightly colored with crisp collars. Each tag sewn into the neck had O.F. written on it. These were all Oliver's hand-me-downs. Even the socks and underwear. Roman forwent the underwear until he secured some of his own and found the darkest thing in the closet: black jeans and a grey silky short sleeve shirt. He pulled on a pair of socks and pocketed the others in his backpack. He tugged on his boots instead of the pointy shoes Oliver had left in the closet.

The last thing he did was reattach his Pada. Resting the device against his forearm, Roman used his free hand and mouth to rip strips of the tape he'd brought for his sphere and pressed them where the Pada met his skin. Putting new tape on felt much better than ripping the old tape off. Sometimes, Roman thought he would rip up his tattoo ink in the process. Once attached, he checked his messages and crypten account. The messages were empty, and the account was full. Just the way he preferred them.

With nothing else to do, Roman exited the bedroom. From below, he heard voices. Oliver and a girl. They were laughing. She sounded happy. Oliver sounded nervous. Something was sizzling, and the smell made Roman's mouth water.

Food and a chance to ruin Oliver's date propelled him down the stairs two at a time.

"Hey Ro," Oliver said when Roman entered the kitchen. His back was to Roman, his hands busy stirring spices into something bubbling atop the stove. "We were just talking about you."

"Yeah?" Roman crossed his arms. "What about?"

"Whether you remembered us trying to make pudding out of mud," the girl said, turning in her seat at the counter to face him.

Liza Flint was not the six-year-old who left the Slums with her family over a decade ago, but she still managed to suck the aggression from Roman's blood all the same. Her straw-like hair had grown into brown locks she wore in braids over her shoulders. Her flour sack dresses had been replaced with some black and purple uniform with a golden crest. She looked like a doll. Something beautiful. Something breakable. She should be contained in some kind of box, not left out to be damaged.

"I remember shoving you into the mud," Roman finally replied.

Liza slid out of her seat and hugged Roman. The action caught him so off guard he stiffened until she stepped away. He should have seen her coming, should have been ready for the attack. She smelled of things he didn't have a name for. The soap in his bathroom was all metal and industrial noise, while what she wore was clean and sweet. It made his stomach growl. He twisted his boot against the floor to ground him back in reality.

"It's good to see you." She smiled. "I'm happy you're here."

Roman was still deciding how he felt about being here. He claimed the seat next to hers, his dark boots planting onto the floor with a thud. Liza slid back into her chair as gently as a breeze. She pulled a can of carbonated water to her and sipped it through a straw. Some women at Dead Dove used this look to get attention and convince someone to buy their next round. Roman didn't know what Liza was trying to convince him to do.

"Do you want it?" Oliver asked, and Roman snapped his attention away from Liza. "Something to drink? Lunch is almost ready."

The heat on the back of Roman's neck dissipated, but his heart did not settle back into a comfortable rhythm until he walked away from Liza and examined the fridge. The coldness of the appliance blasted him, and both the temperature and the stocked shelves surprised him. He couldn't stop staring at the fresh produce, the glass containers of liquids, plastic-wrapped cake slices, bags of portioned vegetables. This was more food than he would see in a week at home, and it was probably the norm up here.

He found a row of colorful soda cans matching Liza's and selected a green one. Beside them was a wooden bowl of fruit. He grabbed an apple and orange, planning to slip them into his coat pocket. When he felt the silk shirt instead of his worn leather jacket, he set them back inside the bowl.

He would stock up on their food before he left. Roman grinned. After saving this place, he'd be able to take whatever he wanted. He'd take entire food stores with him, not just the Flint's refrigerator.

When he sat back at the counter, Oliver set a blue ceramic plate in front of him. Roman recognized the meal instantly. Most nights, it was the only thing any of their parents could scrounge up for them. Oliver and Roman always sharing a plate when the other's caretaker wasn't home. Liza usually slid her portion atop theirs and all three of them shared it like the flour gravy and questionable meat were the best thing in the world.

When they were kids, it probably was.

"Meat on toast?" Roman asked when Oliver set the last component of the dish on his and Liza's plates.

"O's gotten really good at making it," Liza said.

"Probably not as good as your grandma's, but . . ." Oliver trailed off, handing Roman a spoon.

"All of Icaria's food and you make this crap?" Roman took a big bite and followed it with an even bigger spoonful before he swallowed the first.

Oliver's grin was smug. "Doesn't look like you have a problem eating it."

It was better than his grandma's, but Roman wouldn't say it. New flavors erupted with each bite that made his mouth water even while he ate. Something burned his tongue in a pleasurable way, and he wanted to bury his nose in the gravy to understand the smell.

Liza said, "We thought it would be nice to eat something like we used to."

Roman rolled his eyes. Even Liza expected the three of them to be just as they were. Ten years changed everything. The meal may have been the same but elevated just like Oliver and Liza. Roman had climbed and clawed his way to the top of his tiny world, but he was still the same angry kid they left in the trash piles.

"I like your tattoo." Liza's dainty finger rested atop his fist. She traced the head of the viper before pulling back. "No one here has any."

"I have more." Roman hated how the statement blurted out of him. He hated it even more when he added, "If you wanted to see them."

Oliver coughed. "Maybe not in the kitchen."

Liza frowned and focused on her lunch.

Roman finished his in three more bites and soaked up the remaining gravy with his toast. He didn't understand everything in the dish, but he wouldn't complain about the improvement. The gravy wasn't watered down, and he was willing to bet Oliver had used real milk. Roman was pretty sure Oliver knew exactly what kind of meat was in there, too.

"No one eats rats up here, do they?" he asked.

Oliver shook his head. "I don't think there *are* rats up here. Do you want more?"

Oliver ladled more food onto Roman's plate before he could answer. He hovered the serving over Liza's plate, but she shook her head.

"I've got to leave soon." Her eyes darted to the wall clock on the other side of the kitchen.

"Got somewhere better to be with your fancy dress?" Roman asked. She was leaving him again. How soon would it take for Oliver to follow?

She huffed. "My afternoon classes. They're so boring. I wish I could stay here with you guys."

Roman's heart felt uncomfortable again and he blurted out, "I'll go with you." Before Oliver could protest, he added, "Hinge said he wanted people in his school. Might as well start now."

Liza chuckled. "What are you talking about?"

"Roman's not going to your classes," Oliver decided. "You don't have a uniform," he quickly told him.

Roman rolled his eyes, propped his chin in his hand, and kept eating. He yanked the toast off Oliver's plate and dunked it into his gravy. "Whatever."

"We could find you a uniform," Liza said. "Oliver, where's yours?"

"Returned after I graduated."

"Oh yeah," she pouted. "This stinks. It would have been fun if you came with me. Oliver, do I have to go?"

"Yes." Oliver's tone shifted to one of authority, and Liza fell in line with it. "You need to save your sick days for when you're sick."

"You said she was better," Roman snapped at him.

"She still needs to see the doctor to make sure the sickness doesn't come back. Her prosthetic needs recalibrating every six months."

"Guys," Liza interrupted them, and both Roman and Oliver leaned away from the counter. Whatever fight was starting sizzled out between them. "Don't talk about me like I'm not here."

"You need to finish your classes," Oliver said. "We'll be here when you get home." He looked at Roman. "We'll go to the workshop. I have something I want to show you."

"About the . . . project?"

"Yes."

"What project?" Liza asked. "Can I help?"

"You're not getting out of class."

Liza crossed her arms and sank into her chair, looking like the six-year-old girl he used to know.

Roman laughed. "It's all grease monkey shit. You'd hate it."

"Fine." Liza slid from her seat. She shouldered the brown bag hanging off her chair. "But when I get home, we're all going out. Okay?"

"Deal," Oliver answered for him and Roman. "Have fun in class."

"Doubtful," she grumbled, stomping off. Halfway between the kitchen and front door, she stopped and turned around. "See you later, Roman. You better still be here when I get back."

"I'll think about it." Roman hid his smile with the edge of his soda can. He waited for the front door to shut before asking Oliver, "Why doesn't she know about the city failing?"

"You caught that?" Oliver took their finished plates to the sink and ran water over them. Back in the Slums, there would have been a bucket of week-old water for washing dishes. Oliver rinsed each plate under the tap until every speck of gravy washed away. Roman added the water source to his list of things he was taking back with him.

"I'm not an idiot, O."

Oliver sighed, shutting off the water. "No one knows. Except for a few scientists, engineers, and President Hinge's people. He wants to keep the public in the dark."

"He wants to keep them dumb."

"President Hinge doesn't want people to be in a panic," Oliver corrected sternly. "He believes we can fix this discreetly."

"You're one of the scientists, what do you believe?" Roman asked.

"I believe we can fix it. You and I."

Roman crossed his arms. "There was never a mission to get kids into your university, was there?"

"No. I made that up to get you here."

"Why didn't you just ask me?"

Oliver raised an eyebrow. "Would you have come?"

Roman thought for a second and shook his head. "You're right. I would have spit in your face if you asked."

"Exactly." Oliver smiled. "But if I tricked you, made you believe we were looking for someone special . . ."

"I am special," Roman reminded.

"Then let's show them." A spark lit up Oliver's green eyes. "Get your sphere. Let's go to the workshop. You're going to dig it."

Chapter Nine

Roman did *dig it*. He loved everything about the Flint Workshop in the bottom level of the apartment. From the multi-security system at the door, utilizing both digital and mechanical locks, to the brightness of the room established by track lighting on the ceiling, to the huge computer screen on the back wall. All the tables were on locking wheels so they could be moved where they were needed. The longest wall of the room was a pegboard displaying more tools than Roman had ever seen. Half-built constructs lay atop some tables while others had built-in scanning and diagnostic stations like Roman's at Dead Dove.

He ran his ink-stained fingers along the wrenches on the pegboard. They were pure steel. There wasn't a speck of grease or grime on them. On the countertop were clear containers of different-sized screws, bolts, and washers. Each container was labeled with a size and a number that Roman assumed was part of a bigger organization system.

When he discovered the welding station, he whistled low and slow. The device in front of him took his breath away.

"This the Byzing torch?" He didn't need to really ask. He knew it in his bones, but he wanted Oliver's confirmation to make sure he wasn't dreaming. His hands twitched. A primal need to hold the torch overpowered him.

"Newest model." Oliver handed him a pair of thick goggles. "Test it out if you want."

Roman looked from the torch to the goggles to his sphere tucked under his arm. The temptation was making him sweat. He didn't just want to try out the tool; he needed it. He needed to feel its power. He wanted to be as powerful as the red light that could be seen from space. He traded his sphere for the goggles and strapped them over his head.

Everything was pitch-black until he fired on the torch. The blood-red light was as thin as a paper cut, but the force of it vibrated through the device so intensely that Roman felt like he was holding a hornet's nest. It wasn't enough to just hold the torch, to see the flame. Roman needed to use it. He tapped the flame against a nearby table, and it bore a hole as easily as if it had been paper and not professionally-graded steel. Without thinking, Roman sliced the table in half.

He flicked off the Byzing torch and slid the goggles over his head, smiling at his handiwork. The table lay in two perfect halves. The cut steel was still a pure silver color. The torch was too fast, too hot, to even char the metal.

Roman Koa had been King of the Ring, but with the things in this workshop, he could become a god.

He turned to find Oliver, to show him what he'd done, and found him at the computer screen with his sphere plugged into several wires. Data filled the screen.

Roman's blood boiled as if the Byzing torch was set to his skin.

"Hey!" Roman stormed to Oliver, ready to punch him and snatch away his sphere. "What the slant do you think you're doing?"

Oliver stepped out of the way. "I just wanted to see the specs. Calm down, Ro."

Roman picked up his sphere and checked out its exterior. It looked like it should, but Roman still yanked the wires out. As easily as data could be taken from the motherboard, a virus could be inserted too.

"Top-notch, like you said." Oliver nodded, relieved. "Perfect for defeating bots in the arena."

"Yeah, that's what it's designed to do," Roman growled. "What'd you think it was for?"

Oliver shrugged, and his cheery demeanor took over again. "I wanted to see the power level is all."

"You could have just asked."

Oliver looked at the readings on the computer screen. "Ever think about pushing it further?"

"Why?" Roman asked.

"I'm sure you'd think of something to do with it." Oliver turned away from the readouts and leaned against the desk. "But could you?"

"Course I could," Roman boasted. "I'm slanting brilliant, remember?"

"How could I forget?" Oliver tapped the sphere in Roman's arms. "So, why haven't you?"

"Sphere is too small," Roman answered. "Anything bigger and I'd need more than the tiny beams lifting the arena to power the electromagnet."

"It's a magnet?" Oliver asked. He tried covering his shock in wonderment. He dropped his shoulders, finally relaxing.

"What of it?" Roman demanded, uneasy from the change in Oliver's demeanor.

"Nothing," Oliver said softly. "I thought it was a . . . an antigravity thing."

So did a lot of people, but Roman wasn't going to correct anyone and give them an opportunity to best him. It was better people thought he's harnessed the actual antigravity in the Ring's beams instead of using it as a battery. Roman chewed the inside of his cheek. "I thought you wanted to show me something."

"I do." Seeming to remember it now, Oliver led Roman to another table where the skeleton of a robot fighter was laid out. It was humanoid, like the one Franz had used, but with longer limbs ending in mallets. "I started working on this about a month ago, but I could really use your help finishing it."

"No kidding." Roman pinned his sphere between his arm and hip and picked up part of the skeleton. He'd seen junk-yard bots in better shape. "What is this? Aluminum?"

"I wanted it to be fast," Oliver defended.

Roman shook his head. "One sneeze would break this thing. Fast is good but so is surviving a hit. You should be using chrome. At least a chrome alloy."

"I can recast this in chrome," Oliver offered.

"Seventy . . . No, use eighty percent chrome." Roman set his sphere down on the nearest table and took off his borrowed shirt. He could move better in the dark tank beneath. "Where's your blueprint of the exoskeleton? I'll get welding that together."

"You just want to keep using the Byzing torch," Oliver smiled.

"You want my help or not?"

Oliver tapped a few buttons on the side of the table and a hologram blueprint projected in the center of the room. Roman circled it, examining every design point, stretching and shrinking parts with his fingers. It felt like playing with stars.

"I'm making changes," he declared, not impressed with the simple build. It looked too much like Franz's. It looked too much like a sunkisser robot.

Oliver set a crate of parts on the table; metal clinks filled the room. "Do whatever you want, but keep the F."

On the center of the blueprint's chest was the same F that was on the carriage in fancy lettering.

"Your dad really likes showing off the letter?"

"The monogram is mine," Oliver corrected. "I'm the one designing everything."

Roman snapped the goggles over his eyes. "Let's do this."

Hours later, the robot was finished. A seven-foot-tall monster stood in the center of the workshop floor. It looked nothing like Oliver's initial design. Roman had found his inspiration inside a book titled *Encyclopedia C & D*. The Tyrannosaurus Rex was once the scariest dinosaur on the planet with a massive jaw and rows of sharp teeth. Roman fell in love with its hulking body. Oliver liked its fast, whip-like tail.

Roman kept the design skeletal, chrome pieces imitating bones. Circuits flashed red and yellow within the ribs, glowing from head to tail. Oliver wired lighting behind the bot's eyes, so the sockets glowed red like the Byzing torch. The tail ended in a razored edge. Inside the mouth, between the sharp steel teeth, was a cannon designed to fire projectiles. Carved on the snout of the robotic monster was Oliver's monogrammed F and above it was Roman's four-pointed crown.

The king of the dinosaurs was the perfect fit for the king of the Ring.

The T-rex bot was crisp. Every bit of char, and grease, and oil was wiped clean. The same could not be said about Roman and Oliver. The grime Roman had washed off when he first arrived at the house had returned. A stripe of motor oil crossed his forehead and matted his frenzied hair. Each of his pockets had been filled with hand tools or extra screws. The knees of the pants had run thin and ripped from his movements. Oliver's T-shirt was splattered with grease and sweat. He'd tucked a pen behind each ear, and his left hand was wrapped in a bandage from a rogue spark that caught him off guard. They looked like a pair of slummers. They looked like they belonged together.

Roman couldn't keep his eyes off the robot they had built. It was bigger than anything they had designed before. Deadlier than anything they had imagined when they were kids. This bot could stomp, shred, melt, completely obliterate any opponent in the Ring. This bot was only possible because the two of them had combined their skills. Roman's superior hardware knowledge and Oliver's mastery over code.

"What kind of controller were you thinking?" Oliver asked from his seat at the computer. Three empty soda cans were stacked to his left while he worked through a fourth one. His hands flew across the keyboard; he typed nonsense letters against a black screen.

"Something on my Pada," Roman answered.

Oliver didn't look away from his work. "Yours is a bit outdated. I don't know if it will handle this much code."

"But your dinky one can?"

"The processor is small. It's not weak."

Even though Roman was in Icaria, the place where the Pada was invented and probably sold at every corner market and given away at each birthday, he knew he wouldn't be able to afford a new one. He'd been self-upgrading his own for years. He'd make whatever changes were necessary to power this robot.

"Put it on its own controller," Roman decided. He didn't want Oliver having the only access over the robot in case his Pada couldn't handle it.

"Great idea." Oliver snapped his fingers. "I'll add in dead buttons so we can upgrade and add new modes when we want. If we could get this done in an afternoon, just imagine what we could do in a week. A month!"

With the tools and material available to him in this workshop, Roman could see himself designing everything he could dream of. He could see himself being happy.

"How many buttons you want?" Roman asked, eyeing material around the room he could use to fashion the controller.

"Better give me ten."

Roman filled his arms with items from the pegboard and settled into a workstation. He used the Byzing torch to cut through the remaining chrome pieces so the controller would look skeletal too. He added a track pad for movement with a backup analog stick, and ten buttons fitted along the side for easy access. Once completed, he set the controller on Oliver's desk where his soda can had been.

"Nice." Oliver picked up the controller and felt it out. "It looks so cool."

"Yeah." Roman kicked the nearest table leg. He hoped the thudding noise covered his appreciation. If it didn't, Oliver didn't comment on it.

Oliver connected the controller to the computer and the trackpad glowed green, signaling the code download. "It'll be ready to go in a few hours."

Roman leaned against the desk with his back to Oliver. He admired his sleeping robot beast. "Too bad we couldn't take it out now."

Oliver spun around in his chair. "We can take it to the Ring next week at the fight. O'Neal will be surprised to see us working together again."

"The whole slanting Slums will be surprised to see me with a sunkisser like you."

Oliver laughed. "Maybe I can borrow some of your clothes then."

Roman laughed too. "Nah. People will still smell the Icaria on you. You're better off owning up to it."

Oliver took the pens from behind his ears and tapped them against his knee. "I had fun building this with you, Ro."

Roman had too. For a while, grease-covered and talking about robot mechanics, things between them had felt like they did ten years ago. The stranger who brought Roman here was beginning to look like his best friend again. He brought a knuckle to his mouth and then lowered it after ripping the scab off with his teeth.

"What's your plan for the failing gravity beams?" Roman asked, quickly veering away from sentiment before Oliver caught on. "Where do we start?"

Oliver scratched the back of his head. "I thought we could build something to fix it."

"But do you know what needs fixing?"

"Not anymore."

"Anymore?"

Oliver set his mouth into a hard line. If he had an answer for Roman, he wasn't prepared to give it.

Behind them, the computer chimed a noise mimicking a ringing phone. The download screen minimized, and a pop-up window took over the full display with an image of an older man who had the same face shape as Oliver and Liza. Under the photo, the screen read *Christopher Flint Calling*.

"Your dad?" Roman asked. The man in the photo had the same cold eyes he remembered Mr. Flint having. They still made him uncomfortable.

"Yeah." Oliver spun around in a panic, shoving Roman away from the screen.

Roman was about to kick the rolling chair out from under Oliver until he caught a glimpse of something in Oliver's eyes. Roman recognized the expression. Oliver was scared of something.

"Stay out of sight, and don't say a word," Oliver told him. "Please."

Roman rolled his eyes, huffing loudly, but stepped off to the side of the computer. He crossed his arms and nodded at the screen so Oliver would answer the call.

Oliver took a deep breath before doing so, triple-checking that Roman was out of the camera's line of sight.

Oliver accepted the call. "Hey Dad. You home already?"

"Yes, and I noticed the workshop door was locked." Roman couldn't see Mr. Flint's face, but he sounded annoyed. "What are you doing down there?"

"Working on a project; nothing big."

Roman put another knuckle to his mouth. Oliver set his hands in his lap, hiding how he twisted his fingers like he was knotting them up in his lies.

"You didn't show up to work for a small project?"

"I must have lost track of time," Oliver said. "You were right about needing windows in here. Was Mrs. Cordova mad?"

"I smoothed it over." Mr. Flint's words were sharp. Whatever smoothing he did was probably just as sharp.

"I'm really sorry Dad; I'll go see her first thing in the morning and apologize."

"You're to fill out a reprimand card before you do."

"Of course."

"I'll bring it down. Let me see this pet project that was so important to you."

Oliver paled. "I'll come up! You don't need to come down here. It's a wreck after today. Plus, the bot isn't finished yet."

"A fighting bot?" Mr. Flint asked with distaste. Apparently, ten years hadn't changed his opinion on the sport. Both Roman's and Oliver's backsides had paid the price whenever Mr. Flint caught them sneaking into the Ring.

Oliver twisted his fingers. "A mowing bot. I was thinking of something to help maintain the lawns. I know you said the current operation does a bad job of it."

Mr. Flint must have bought the lie because Oliver relaxed slightly. He flattened out his hands atop his knees.

"Alright. Meet me in the study. You can tell me more about this build while filling out the card."

"Yes, sir. See you in a minute." Oliver ended the call and collapsed in his chair with a heavy sigh.

"What was that?" Roman asked.

Oliver ran a hand down his face, smearing some grease over his cheek. "Nothing."

"Seems like your dad still hates ro-battles." Roman moved out of his hiding spot.

"Even more since we got here. Dad hates everything related to the Slums now."

"Your dad doesn't know I'm here, does he?"

Oliver looked at him, exhaustion tugging his features down. "You really are slanting brilliant, Ro."

"Tell me what's going on," Roman demanded. "Or I'm going to tell everyone about the grav problems."

Roman had no idea how he'd spread the news about the city falling without being sent back to the Slums and labeled a liar, but his threat was enough to make Oliver leap from his seat.

"Don't do that." Oliver blocked Roman from the exit. "You can't do that."

Roman raised his fists, ready to fight, and Oliver laid his hands over them. He didn't react to the blood congealing across Roman's knuckles.

"Listen Ro, stay here," Oliver said. "Play around with whatever you want, and when I come back, I'll tell you everything."

"What's in it for me?"

Oliver groaned. "I'll get you a Byzing Torch."

Roman smiled his serpentine smile. "And a new Pada."

"And a new Pada," Oliver agreed. "Do we have a deal?"

Roman sat in the rolling chair and propped his boots atop the desk. "Don't make me wait long."

Chapter Ten

Sometime later, the workshop door opened, and Roman looked up from the mess of scrap metal he was working on. In his wait for Oliver, he'd managed to piece together three tiny robots. They were each as tall as his hand. One resembled him with ink-stained chrome and wild pointy edges. Another looked like Oliver: aluminum body with wheels for feet. The final one was for Liza. This one possessed the strongest defenses. The skirt Roman fashioned had a lace-like patterned thanks to an hour's work with the Byzing Torch.

It wasn't Oliver who entered the workshop, though. Liza shut the door behind her and skipped over to Roman. She'd changed out her school uniform for a purple dress with too many bows. They hung off the fabric and threatened to catch on table edges.

"Hey there." She smiled at him. "What are you working on?"

Roman scooted back from the table to show off his work. "Little fighting bots."

"They're cute," Liza squealed. She picked up the ink-stained one and turned it over in her hands before picking up the aluminum one. "These look like you and O. Wait. Is this one me?"

Blushing, Roman barked, "What about it?"

"I like it." Liza held her bot to the side of her face, letting Roman compare his creation to the real thing. "She looks just like me."

"Robots don't have genders." It was all Roman could say, and he felt stupid for saying it.

Liza playfully shoved his shoulder. "Do they work?"

"Yeah."

"Let's rooooooooo-battle then. Where's the controller?"

Roman crossed his arms. A grin pulled at his lips. "You battle?"

She leaned over to stare him in the eyes. It was like a mouse squaring up to a lion. "How hard can it be?"

"For me, it's as easy as breathing. For you?" Roman shrugged.

"I'm going to make you eat those words." Liza straightened and set her bot on the table across from the one that resembled Roman. "Turn them on, let's go."

Roman did as requested. He didn't mind being bossed around by her for some reason. Even as kids, Liza had possessed a power over Roman he'd never understood. If the neon underside of Icaria was his sun, then she had been his warmth.

Once powered on, the tiny fighter's faceplates lit up and chirped, signaling they were ready. Roman held his Pada over his. "Do the same with yours," he instructed. "It will connect to your Pada and the controls will come up. They're basic, perfect for a beginner."

She ignored his taunt and rammed her bot against his as soon as the pairing completed. Roman admired her tenacity, but that wouldn't win her the match. He knew his bot couldn't break her defensive shell, so he used the terrain to his advantage. In thirty seconds, her bot was on the floor and his was circling the table in a victory lap.

"No fair," Liza said, scooping her robot off the floor. She held his creation as if it were alive. A tiny soul cupped in her gentle hands.

"Life's not fair," Roman replied.

"Is Oliver down here?" Liza glanced around the workshop. "I was hoping you boys would be ready to go exploring."

Roman shook his head. "O's with your dad. Guess he got in trouble not going to work or something."

Liza frowned. "He's never missed a day in his life. They should be nicer to him."

"His boss?"

"And our dad," she answered. "He never gives Oliver any slack. No matter what he does, Dad thinks he can do it better. He said that since we're not from here originally then we have to prove we belong here every day."

"Does your dad know I'm here?" Roman asked, hoping to get a more concrete answer from her.

Liza examined her robot, buffing away a scratch with the hem of her dress. "I don't think he does."

"Why not?"

"O told me to keep it a secret."

Liza refused to look at him, keeping all of her focus on her little robot. If it were anyone else, Roman would have ripped it out of her hands and demanded real answers. But Liza wasn't like anyone else.

Roman asked another question, "What about your mom?"

Liza rubbed her thumb against the robot harder and faster. "Mom died a while ago."

"I didn't know."

"How would you have?" Liza set down her robot and pinned him with a sad smile. "I'm not sad or anything. I know she's hanging out with your grandma now."

"And my mom," Roman gave away freely.

Liza laid her hand against Roman's tattooed forearm. He flinched under her soft hands, but she didn't move away from him or his trapped, animal snarl. She squeezed his arm; it was the closest thing Roman had had to a hug in years. It made him think of his mother. Of how he was powerless to save her. Of how he had vowed he'd never feel like that again.

Roman pulled his arm away and watched his robot circle the table.

"Hanging with your mom, too." Liza added.

"Yeah." Roman grabbed his robot before it completed another lap around the table and powered it down. The only way to leave the Slums was death, and, to make that fact a little easier to swallow, the slummers believed that after death, people elevated to their own floating city. Families and friends would be reunited there, a place with clear skies and good food. A place for living, not just surviving. No yellow robes required.

If that place did exist, Roman hoped his and Liza's moms were spending their evenings together again, passing the night with stories and stitching clothing together to sell in the market. On the darkest nights, Roman swore he heard his mom humming a song he didn't remember the name of.

"If O's going to be busy the rest of the night," Liza said, "how about you and I go exploring?"

"Just us?" His mother's song faded from his mind. His throat tightened in a way he hadn't felt since his first official arena match.

"I'm sure you want to see Icaria, right?" Liza asked. "We don't have to wait for Oliver. I know plenty of cool spots to take you."

Roman had made Oliver a promise to stay in the workshop, but it felt wrong to deny Liza this simple request.

Roman had never been good at keeping promises, anyway.

"Where are we going?" Roman asked after he and Liza snuck out of the apartment and stepped onto the street with all the matching buildings.

Liza looked over her shoulder at him but didn't stop moving. "I was thinking we'd get a drink and then go to the park. You haven't seen a sunset before. It's the best place to see it. On the edge."

"The edge?" It sounded ominous. A dangerous place.

"The edge of the city."

The edge of the disk suspended above a sea of acid-saturated clouds. Very dangerous indeed. Roman would need a glass of stardust to relax at a place like that. He found it fitting that the sunkissers would enjoy watching the acid clouds that kept his home a prison.

Liza fell back a step and slid her arm through his. Roman's senses seized. His brain shut down. If he were a bot in the ring, he'd be a prime target for a knockout blow. After an internal reboot, he felt the warmth of her skin through the silk of his shirt. The smell of her perfume assaulted his nose. She tugged him across the street, dodging carriages and other pedestrians. Other couples their age walked along the sidewalks in a similar way, joined at the arm.

After a young man locked eyes with Roman, he attempted to slide his arm out of Liza's, but she tightened hers to keep him trapped. Like in the workshop, he didn't want to fight her. It was a comfortable jail, so Roman stopped his attempt. He felt a rapid heartbeat where her fingers splayed across his arm, and he wasn't sure who it belonged to.

"What is it you smell like?" he asked trying to ignore the sickening sensation.

Liza looked up at him. She was even shorter than Oliver. "You like it?"

"It's okay." Roman kept his face forward.

"It's daffodils."

"What?"

Liza giggled. "They're a type of flower. Bright yellow, kind of looks like a trumpet. I like how they smell. I sometimes forget how bad the Slums were. How ugly it was. That there aren't any flowers growing."

Roman grumbled, "It's not a place for pretty things."

She laughed again, and Roman realized he liked the sound. "Maybe that's why we all had to leave."

Roman pulled his arm from her grasp. He really needed that drink.

The route they traveled was almost identical to the one Oliver had led him down earlier. Roman's breath burned in his throat, fearing Liza was taking him, his ugliness, back to the elevation platform. When they didn't arrive there, Roman realized it was just how Icaria looked. Everything was uniform and crisp. Tall buildings stretching into the darkening sky like guards for a palace. There were more people out at this hour, more carriages moving along the streets. Everyone wore colorful outfits and carried conversations that kept them distracted and carefree. Roman could have robbed at least a dozen people if he were alone.

Liza chatted casually beside him, pointing out locations in between her stories about her day. University sounded dreadfully boring and full of annoying people. He was glad he didn't go with her.

"What are you studying?" Roman asked when she took a breath. "Oliver said people can choose what they learn?"

"Yeah, after your sixth year you can pick a specialty. I picked medicine."

"You want to be a doctor?"

"Someone that can help people," Liza clarified. "Like the staff that got me healthy again."

"Oliver said you were going to die." She flinched beside him and then tucked her arm through his again. "I didn't know it was that bad. When you left, you just had a cough."

"It was part of something worse," she said. "The disease was attacking my organs, the coughing meant it was in my lungs. It was in my kidneys when we got here."

"Did the treatment hurt?"

Liza shook her head. "I was knocked out for most of it. The bruising around my sides hurt the most. And the needles, but once the medicine was in my blood, I started feeling better."

"But it can come back?"

"I'm more likely to get it since I had it before." She patted her side. "The device helps keep my body clean, though."

"Your prosthetic lung?"

"And kidney."

It didn't make sense to Roman. Replacing an arm with a metal one was an easy concept to understand. It was just replacing a part on a robot. He couldn't wrap his head around replacing an organ with a prosthetic one. There were too many complications. Too many moving parts to account for. He eyed Liza's chest and stomach where the prosthetics would be. Did she have scars, he wondered? Or did the doctor include zippers so they could access the new parts for repairs? How long would the prosthetics keep her alive? He chewed his lip since he couldn't bring his knuckles to his mouth.

"Roman?" Liza asked.

"Yeah?"

"You're staring."

Roman's face flushed with heat, and he ripped his gaze away from her. He hadn't been staring at her body, just her insides, but that didn't sound any better when he realized he was thinking of dissecting her.

"How did you get it?" he asked, unsure how to move forward. "Get sick?"

Liza shrugged. "I think just living in the Slums. People there are sick all the time. I just wasn't strong enough to fight it off myself."

Roman slid out of her grasp again. He'd been able to fight off the other kids, the rats, and some nights the hunger, but he couldn't protect her from an illness. Just like he couldn't protect his mother.

"Ro, will you stop?" Liza faced him, hands on her hips. "There's nothing wrong with us holding hands. You are escorting me. It's totally normal up here."

"I could be carrying a disease."

She rolled her eyes and said, "You were decontaminated when you got here, right?"

"Yeah."

Liza slid her arm back around his. "Then you're fine."

Roman didn't think thirty seconds in a glass box could remove all the filth of the Slums, but he stopped fighting her. Liza's tenacity didn't seem limited to robot fights. He let her lead him down another street to a building marked with a pink and white striped awning.

"This is my favorite place," she said, opening the door.

"You can get a drink here?" Roman asked skeptically. He knew Icaria was different, but he figured he'd recognize a bar.

The inside was too bright to be a bar, though. The floors too clean, the air too sweet smelling. As they approached the counter, Roman eyed the menu hanging on the wall behind it. He didn't recognize any of the drinks, but he was certain none contained alcohol.

"This is a bar?" he asked her.

Liza laughed loudly enough that the pair ahead of them turned to stare at her. She paid them no attention. "No, goofball. This is a coffee shop. We're not old enough to drink alcohol. Did you think we were going to a bar?"

Roman crossed his arms and grumbled, "You said we were getting a drink."

Liza was still giggling. "Yeah, an iced coffee or something. Ro, you crack me up."

Roman silently tried to figure out why he was becoming the butt of her jokes as well as Oliver's. Were all slummers this funny to a sunkisser or was he an easy target to make fun of? A girl a little older than Liza greeted them when they stepped to the counter. Her pink-and-white apron matched the awning.

"Hey, Liza," the girl said. Her eyes kept flicking to Roman, who kept glowering. "Your usual?"

"You know it," Liza answered, tapping the Pada watch around her wrist to the crypten transfer screen on the counter.

"And for your . . . friend?" The girl raised her eyebrows at Liza.

"What do you want, Roman?" Liza asked.

He didn't know. Nothing on the menu sounded good. "Give me what Liza's getting."

"Okay," the girl tapped a few keys on the cash register, "two iced mocha chip coffees with whip cream. To go?"

"Yeah," Liza answered. "Roman's taking me to see the sunset."

The girl gasped, her eyes darting between the two of them. "Really?"

Liza nodded and tapped her Pada against the cash register to complete the crypten transfer. A triumphant smile painted her face, and Roman didn't know what fight he had just been a part of.

The girl leaned across the counter and whispered to Liza, "You have to tell me everything tomorrow. Actually, call me tonight."

"I don't know, Sherry," Liza said. "We'll probably be out all night."

Sherry blinked at Liza, her mouth opening into a wide *O*. The other worker placed their drinks on the counter. Liza grabbed them both and headed out the door with Roman in tow. He was happy to leave the shop. Roman accepted the drink and took a quick sip of it through the pink straw. It was so cold and sweet that his back teeth ached and his head spasmed. He yanked the straw from his mouth and grabbed his forehead.

"Brain freeze?" Liza asked with a grin.

"A what?" Roman managed through clenched teeth.

"A brain freeze, it happens when you drink something cold too fast." Liza took a slow drag from her straw. "Press your tongue to the roof of your mouth. It'll make it go away faster."

Roman did as directed and was relieved when the pain subsided. When it was gone, he took a slower sip. The ache in his teeth remained, but at least his head had stopped screaming.

"What is this park we're going to?" he asked her.

"It's just a park," Liza answered. "Think I'm lying to you?"

"I think we know different things by the same name," he answered. "That girl didn't act like it was a normal park."

"Sometimes couples go there to make out." Liza said quickly, popping her straw back in her mouth the moment the words were out.

"I'm not your boyfriend."

"I know that," she said, "but other people can assume whatever they want."

Roman rolled his eyes, and they continued their journey in silence. Liza didn't slide her arm through his until the sidewalk turned to flat rocks and the buildings thinned into a green field. Colorful flowers that he didn't know the names of grew in patches along the pathway. In a circle lined by three benches, a fountain bubbled and a few birds flapped in the spray. It was all beautiful, but not what captured his attention. At the edge of the disk, where the grass fell away to nothingness, sat an orange orb.

The sun that had burned him earlier today was now a dying god. Its brightness gasping for life, its heat nothing more than a faraway echo. It dipped into a roaring ocean of dark clouds, the sky above it a mess of colors.

"I knew you'd love it," Liza said with a grin. "Let's get closer. Sometimes it'll make rainbows with the acid."

Roman followed her down the path, desperately speeding around corners whenever a tree blocked his view of the horizon. Liza took him to a bench overlooking the edge, and they sat. The failing light caused sparks of colors inside the acid clouds. At the slightest breeze, Roman recognized the smell coming off them. It burned his nose hairs, and he felt defenseless sitting this close to the skin-melting rain. Where the disk dropped off, the grass was dry and brown. A silky fog lapped over the edge like a wave.

The sun continued to dip below the cloud layer until it vanished with just the promise it would raise again tomorrow.

Soft glowing streetlights lit up the park.

"Why wouldn't you be my boyfriend?" The way Liza blurted the question, Roman figured she'd been thinking about it since the coffee shop.

It still made Roman choke on his drink. "What are you talking about?"

"Now that you're here," she repeated. "Why won't you? Just because we moved didn't mean I stopped having a crush on you."

"You had a crush on me?" Roman blinked owlishly.

"Wasn't it obvious?"

To Roman, anything she did should have been obvious, but, like the sun, she was painful to look at for too long. "I guess I missed the signs."

"Well, this is embarrassing now." Liza fidgeted with her hands. The action was oddly similar to Oliver's, but Roman didn't think she was lying. "I kind of thought you liked me back. Please don't tell O about this, okay?"

"Liza, I'm not staying here," Roman said, not wanting to correct her assumption of how she thought he felt.

Even if they were both in the Slums, Roman would never feel like he deserved a love like Liza. She was pure starlight. He was a black hole. He'd devour her without even knowing the damage. The Slums wasn't a place for love. Roman wasn't the boy for love, either.

"You're not staying?!" Liza almost shouted. "But why? The Slums are disgusting. It's so much better up here! Why won't you stay?"

"Oliver brought me here for a job," he explained simply. "After it's done, I have to finish things at home."

Roman needed to take everything Icaria had to the Slums.

"And you won't come back after you've done all that?"

"I don't know." If Liza thought the Slums were disgusting, how long would it take for her to think of Roman the same way?

"Well, you should think about it," she said. "O and I really missed you."

Roman couldn't say the same. He'd spent the last ten years hating them. He finished his drink and tossed the cup over the edge. A violent hissing filled the air as the acid dissolved it.

"What else is there to do here?" he asked, almost jealous of the cup's violent departure from the situation.

"There's a skating rink we can go to. It's black-out night, so all the neon lights will be on."

Roman shook his head. "I have neon lights at home."

"But not a skating rink." Liza pleaded. "Come on, it'll be a lot of fun. It's easy to do too if you're scared because it's your first time."

"I'm not scared." Roman stood. "Let's go."

Liza tossed her cup over the edge with a reckless grin and leapt from her seat.

She picked up her babbling as they exited the park, talking about her first time skating and how her friends would go every week when classes were on break. It was easy to let her voice carry him along, not needing to listen to every word but letting it become part of Icaria. As the city darkened. every street corner was illuminated by a lamppost shining softly.

The lights, the people, everything in Icaria was soft compared to the Slums. If the city's gravity did fail and it did crash, Roman knew the sunkissers wouldn't last a day without all their luxuries. Part of him wanted it to collapse just to teach them a lesson. The Slums would live on. They had survived when the rich and powerful left them to die after Icaria's completion. The slummers would find another way.

Liza's skating rink was a perfectly square building with music pouring from the windows. When she opened the door, colored light fell across the sidewalk. She pulled Roman inside. The rink was full of people. The energy oozing off them felt like the kind Roman felt at the Ring. A room packed with people could encourage a lot of bad things to happen. Roman kept close to Liza, looming above her whenever possible and scowling at anyone who tried approaching.

"Chill out, Ro," she said, looking up at him with a grin. "There's nothing dangerous here. Well, except maybe you. Stay here. I'm going to get our skates."

She merged into the crowd standing in a ring outside the room's circular center. The floor shifted from carpet to wood, and everyone seemed to understand an unspoken rule that the wooden floor was for skating and the carpeted floor for walking. Roman watched the skaters whizz across the floor on their wheeled shoes. It looked fun. Some completed turns, some leapt through the air, and some locked elbows with others to sling-shot them across the floor.

"Who let you out of the garbage bin?" asked a voice behind Roman.

Roman fell into the growing energy, feeling his blood electrify at the chance of confrontation. He turned to face his opponent. Franz Eddison didn't look any different from the night at the Ring, except now he had an array of people at his back. They were as intimidating as his humanoid robot fighter.

"That bot you melted was worth a lot of cryptens and you're going to pay it back."

Roman crossed his arms lazily as Franz approached him. "I'm not going to pay for your stupidity. Next time, don't come to the Ring unless you're ready."

"You used illegal tech and you're going to admit it."

"Are you going to make me?" Roman leaned down eye-to-eye to the sunkisser.

Franz readied a punch that made Roman laugh. It was clear that he had never thrown one before. The sunkisser would break his thumb before dealing any damage.

"I'll give you the first hit." Roman turned his face so Franz had a perfect view of his cheek.

Franz's cheerleaders shouted encouragement at him, and other people in the crowd turned to see the commotion. Franz threw his punch, and it landed on the bottom of Roman's jaw with about as much force as a butterfly.

"My turn." Roman sucker punched Franz in the gut and as he doubled over spitting on the ground, Roman bashed his knee into Franz's chin. The sunkisser fell to his knees and Roman eyed his friends. "Anyone else think they can make me admit a lie?"

One of them lunged forward, and Roman met the assault with a fist to his nose. The sunkisser crumbled to the ground. Franz returned to his feet, surprising Roman, and ran the back of his hand against his bloody lip. He attempted the same move as his buddy and Roman easily raised his leg and kicked Franz in the chest.

"Don't get up this time." Roman offered the advice with a smirk.

Franz sat on the ground, looking up at Roman. The sunkisser's bottom lip was split open and his face was cherry-red as he tried sucking in air. The friend who Roman had punched in the face had blood pouring down his broken nose and over his chin. The second one couldn't hold Roman's gleeful stare.

Franz's other friends picked them off the floor, and they tumbled through the crowd and out of the door. Roman sighed and straightened his shirt. This was the second-best thing to happen tonight. The first being the robot dinosaur waiting for him back at the workshop. Roman turned and found Liza staring at him across the crowd, her hand over her mouth and her eyes wide. She looked horrified. His stomach dropped.

She dropped the two pairs of skates she was holding and stormed out of the building. The crowd erupted into murmurs. They pointed at Roman. Over the music, he heard "slummer" and "bully" and "whack job."

Not once did Roman hear "king." He cursed and followed Liza, the crowd parting for him like the giant rat he was.

Chapter Eleven

It wasn't hard to find Liza when Roman exited the skating rink. She stood across the street talking to Franz. His posse hovered a few paces behind them, lurking in the streetlights. One had their hands braced on either side of the other's broken nose. Neither of them moved forward with trying to reset it. Roman leaned against the rink and watched their interactions. It looked like Liza was apologizing. She touched Franz's arm, and he reacted like the touch was normal. That it was familiar. It made Roman uncomfortable. Liza pulled a white cloth from her dress pocket and dabbed it against his bottom lip, cleaning away the blood.

Franz looked across the street and whatever kindness he showed Liza vanished when his eyes landed on Roman. The sunkisser's eyes burned with the same intensity they had the night at the Ring.

Roman used a fingernail to pick something out between his teeth. He didn't need to show off for the sunkisser. Both Franz's robot and physical blows were easy to counter and boring. If there was a rematch, Roman would make sure he didn't stand back up.

Franz turned back to Liza and tossed her cloth at her feet. He pointed his finger at her chest and started talking. Even from his distance, Roman saw Liza's bottom lip quiver. No matter how long they'd been apart, the need to protect her overpowered Roman's brain functions.

Roman pushed off the wall and crossed the street in quick strides. Franz's posse shuffled back a few feet as he approached, but Franz was too slow. Roman grabbed the hand pointing at Liza and squeezed Franz's fingers until the knuckles popped. Franz's entire frame squirmed in response.

"Go away," Roman ordered, dropping his hand.

Franz wrapped his good hand around the fingers Roman had crushed. He looked past Roman to address Liza. "Your slum colors are showing, Liza. Next time we have a disagreement, be civil and talk it over with me. Don't sic your junkyard dog on me, got it?"

"Yes." Liza's voice trembled.

Roman glared at Franz until he retreated to his group, and they walked away. He picked Liza's cloth off the ground and handed it to her. His stomach twisted into a mess of tangled wires when he saw her. Makeup had smudged under both of her eyes and more of it ran down her cheeks in smokey gray rivers.

"Liza?" Roman prompted her as gently as he could. The hiss from a soldering gun would have sounded nicer.

"Why are you such a bully?" Liza's voice was watery, her tears shaking her throat. She shoved Roman's shoulder.

"He made you cry?" Roman was still trying to understand whatever he had witnessed. Why was this third-rate robot fighter hanging around Liza?

"No, he didn't."

Roman didn't need to see her hands fidgeting just like Oliver's to know she was lying. She used the cleaner half of the cloth to wipe away her makeup and blow her nose. Her face was still smudgy, but at least she sounded drier.

"Why'd you have to go pick a fight like that?" she asked.

Roman snorted. "Your buddy came for me first."

"So, you hit him?"

Roman shrugged. "He didn't seem like the talking type."

Liza gasped, her hands flying up in frustration. "Franz is the head of our debate team and president of Young Leaders of Icaria Education. All he does is talk!"

Roman didn't know what either of those things meant, but neither title impressed him. "He must've used up all his words."

"Let's just go home," Liza sighed. "I'm going to have to find a way to clean this up."

Roman grabbed her wrist before she turned away from him. "Liza, are you scared of this guy?"

"What if I was? Would you go beat him up again?" She shook her hand until Roman released her. "That's not how you deal with things here, Ro. This isn't the Slums."

Roman slid his hands into his pockets and started down the street. He didn't need her to remind him of what he already knew. He didn't need her to remind him he wasn't cut out for a place like this. Roman had left the Slums, but it couldn't leave him, no matter how long he stayed in a decontamination chamber. He needed to get back with Oliver, solve the gravity problem, and go back home. With the technology here, he could better the Slums and run a monopoly on the luxuries while guaranteeing the basics. No more dirty water. No more rotten food. No more sickness.

"Ro!" Liza ran after him, her heels clipping against the sidewalk with each step. "Ro, wait up. Roman, slow down."

He let her catch up to him and stared her down until she spoke. She had the same green eyes as Oliver. He'd never noticed before.

"You're going the wrong way." She didn't hold his stare; her eyes kept dropping to the ground. She sounded like someone should when addressing the King of the Ring. Nervous, never sure if he would strike out like the viper inked against his hand. "There's a shortcut through this street, come on."

Roman followed Liza down a few more identical streets. He almost missed the feeling of her arm tucked in his. He almost traced back through the night to see where everything went wrong. He almost wanted to apologize. Not for hitting Franz, but for whatever made Liza lose her tenacity. Instead, Roman focused on the road, unsure of how anyone could find their way in a maze like this. The street they were on opened to a small courtyard with another fountain that matched the one in the park, including the benches and flowers. Without the sun to guide them toward the sky, the blooms dropped. A display board cycled through notices on the far side of the yard. Roman didn't care about any of the displays. Each slide was another way for Icaria to brag.

Until the last one slid into view. Roman stopped abruptly. Liza gasped at his side.

Roman's photo was on the display. The picture was from a fight at the Ring. Judging by the wicked grin, he had just won the match. He looked reckless and mad. A wild animal unleashed from a cage. Under the photo it read: *Roman Koa. Wanted for crimes against Icaria. Extremely dangerous. Do not approach. Call Icaria Enforcement if spotted.*

"For hitting that slanting sunkisser?" Roman barked. He tried flicking the poster away, but his fingers passed through the hologram. It was shoddy work compared to Oliver's deer.

"We need to go." Liza grabbed his hand, pulling him down a street. "Right now!"

Roman heard sirens before they exited the small alley. When they emerged on the connecting street, red lights flashed across the buildings. A carriage with a black stripe squealed to a stop, blocking off part of the street. Roman shoved Liza away from him, back into the shadows of the alley.

"Run," he told her. "Go home and don't come back."

"Roman." She reached for him, her dainty hand turning red as the searchlights passed the alley.

"Run," he said again and then bolted in the other direction.

Boots thundered after him as Icaria enforcers began their chase. Roman didn't know the streets, but he turned at every corner he came across. If he could get lost in the city, then he could wait out the chase. But there was no place for him to hide. Streetlights peppered every dark corner. His heart started to burn from the exertion. On his right, the ladder of a fire escape hung above a garbage can. He leapt onto the can and grabbed the bottom rung. He shimmied up the ladders and platforms until he reached the top. Cold brick soaked through his silk shirt, and he relished in the relief. Below him, the enforcers continued down the street followed by two carriages. Their flashing red lights painted everything in swatches of red.

It reminded Roman of the flashes of light at the Ring after a robot was defeated. His eagerness for the fight caused the iced coffee in his stomach to rock around. He leaned into the feeling. This was just another night in the arena, except now he was the robot fighting for his life.

Roman rolled back his shirt sleeve to access his Pada. He opened the messaging application to send one to Oliver. Before the keyboard loaded, a spotlight submerged Roman in blinding light. He shielded his eyes with the back of his hand and looked up. An aircraft hovered above him, whipping his hair and drowning him in sound. The side door of the craft opened. The end of a rifle aimed at his chest. A tiny red dot confirmed the target.

Roman wished he was as heartless as people seemed to think him to be.

He slammed himself into the ladder and slid down to the next level while the gunman opened fire. The bullets ricocheted on metal, louder than the actual rifle. A bullet slid through the top platform's grated flooring and embedded an inch from Roman's boot. He couldn't stop to admire the aiming software or theorize how he could incorporate it into a robot build. He scrambled down the other levels and collapsed into the garbage can when he dropped off the last rung.

When he pushed off the ground, a boot kicked his side, sending him back into the garbage that had just spilled. Another kick to his back kept him down while someone sat on his back, wrestling his hands behind him, and binding them into handcuffs. It happened so fast. Roman had just recovered from falling into the trash when he was yanked up by his bound hands and hair.

Icaria enforcers surrounded him. Each wore the standard white uniform of a city employee, but they had added touches: black helmets and black utility belts sporting baton sticks, tasers, handcuffs, and other things Roman didn't have names for. He struggled against the cuffs and the hand atop his head snarled into his hair. He was met with a surprise blow to the back of the head. Roman's vision spotted and hot pain seared the back of his eyes as his head involuntarily fell forward.

One enforcer lifted his chin with the end of his baton. Roman saw his reflection in the helmet's visor. He looked like the picture on his wanted poster: unhinged and dangerous, except now he was in chains.

"Roman Koa, you are under arrest for your crimes against Icaria."

Roman barked a laugh. "All this fuss over some sunkisser like Franz Eddison? Slant it all."

Several of the enforcers' helmets moved side to side as they looked at one another. One of them clasped a new pair of cuffs around Roman's ankles.

The enforcer with the baton at his chin asked, "Are you admitting to another crime?"

"I ain't admitting to nothing I didn't do." Roman spat on the enforcer's boot.

The last thing Roman saw was the side of the baton slamming against his cheek.

Chapter Twelve

The Slums, a disgusting and lawless place, didn't have a prison. Slummers solved their problems on their own. If someone wronged somebody, then it was up to them to figure it out. Most things followed a balance and could be solved with some kind of payment. Roman found it funny that the righteous Icaria had constructed a prison when they were supposed to be better than the slummers.

He pressed his bruised cheekbone against the cold floor of his cell. He hadn't seen anyone since he woke up alone in the three by five room. There was a short mattress in the back corner and a toilet opposite it. The cell pushed down on Roman on all sides. He was too tall for a place like this. If he laid down on the mattress, his feet stuck through the cell bars at the front. If he stretched out his arms, his knuckles dragged against the cinderblock walls. If he stood, the top of his head brushed the ceiling.

Roman didn't know how long he'd been knocked out. While he was unconscious, his clothing had been replaced with an orange jumpsuit. His last name was printed across the chest along with a four-digit number. His Pada had been ripped from his arm, the tape leaving a perfect outline. Roman scratched at it in between fits of useless and uncomfortable sleep to remove the sticky residue. He hadn't been brought any food or water, but he wasn't expecting any comfort from his captors.

Sometime later, footsteps filled the narrow hallway outside the cell bars. Roman's cheek had stopped pulsing, and the swelling was less tender, so he imagined at least twelve hours had passed since he first awoke. Roman didn't move from his seat on the mattress, his back to the wall and eyes closed against the constant glare of the overhead lights.

Someone banged against the cell bars to get his attention. Roman waited until they started shouting his name—and other rude things—before he opened one eye to check out his company. The enforcer banged his baton against the cell even harder. The man beside him looked proud to have Roman trapped in a cage.

"Wake up inmate," the enforcer said in between hits. "President Hinge doesn't have all day to wait on you."

President Hinge's graying hair was slicked away from his oily forehead. He was younger than Roman assumed he'd be. Too young to have gray hair and wrinkles. Roman snickered thinking about what kind of stress could leave such age marks on a sunkisser. Maybe his steak was always too rare, or his fancy house had too many stairs, or he stayed up too late counting all his cryptens. Over his ugly burnt-orange suit and tie, Hinge wore a white coat like Oliver's but his had a different patch.

Roman shut his eye. "He'll be waiting longer."

The president scoffed at Roman's remark.

"Don't worry sir," the enforcer said, the jangling of keys interrupting his sentence. "I'll get him in a cooperative mood."

"Don't bother," President Hinge said. "He's responsible for the failing gravity stations. With Koa here, they'll return to normal."

Roman whipped his head toward the president. The rapid movement caused both Hinge and the enforcer to flinch. "You think I'm causing the power shortage?"

"Who else has a robot capable of accessing the gravity beams?" President Hinge asked, but his tone didn't leave room for an answer. "Don't bother denying it. We've seen you do it enough during your little robot battles. Your days of harassing Icaria are over."

"My sphere doesn't do that!" Roman shouted. He leapt from the mattress toward the cell door, wishing he could smack the grin off the president's face. "Run your own specs. Flint has the report."

"Oliver, yes, he should be coming to my office today." President Hinge spoke more to the enforcer than to Roman. "Did you know he offered to go to the Slums and pick up Koa instead of me having to send a troop? Saved me a ton of cryptens and bad press."

President Hinge laughed, and the enforcer joined him. Roman's blood boiled so badly he couldn't hear anything beside the roaring in his ears. Oliver had sold him out. Oliver had dragged him up here, made him build the best robot fighter he ever had, and then gotten rid of him.

Roman knew there was a catch to the job; there always was.

Rage overtook Roman. Despite everything he'd done for himself, despite every trash heap he'd climbed out of, despite every fight he'd won, he was still an angry kid. He tore through the cell like a tornado, tossing the pillow, itchy blanket, and mattress against a wall. He kicked against the concrete floor. He punched the cinderblock walls.

"Slummers," President Hinge commented to the enforcer loud enough for Roman to hear. "They're nothing but barbaric rats."

Roman whirled on the cell bars, a punch aimed for Hinge's wrinkled and ugly face. He'd tear the president's smug grin off his lips and toss the bloody remains at the enforcer. They hadn't seen barbaric yet. But the enforcer pulled Hinge back before Roman's fist could land and bashed his baton against Roman's hand. A scab burst open, and blood smeared across the baton. Roman ignored the pain.

President Hinge straightened his burnt-orange suit, his face matching the color. Part of his hair had fallen from its hold. He didn't need spraypainted fangs and horns to look like a demon when he did so well enough on his own. Roman glared at him as the enforcer escorted Hinge down the hallway.

Anger pulsed through him, lighting every nerve on fire. He knew who he wanted to direct this rage at, but Oliver wasn't here to take the brunt of it. Nothing had changed in the ten years he was gone, or in the last few days they'd been together. Oliver had left him again. Oliver had left Roman to rot like the trash Oliver probably thought he was. Roman needed to hit something, but with nothing in the cell, his anger and rage and betrayal imploded inward like a dying star. When his anger ate through his energy reserve, he collapsed on the overturned mattress and let exhaustion pull him under.

Roman's eyes fluttered open, and he stared at the white wall of his cell. The overhead lights never turned off, and he was lost in the forever false daylight. His legs and arms burned from their cramped positions. His knuckles stung from his earlier assault on himself, and his pinky swelled from the enforcer's baton. He was still so angry. He put one of his knuckles against his teeth and rolled onto his back, his legs bending at the knees to keep them within the cell walls.

This was his life now. Imprisoned for a crime he didn't commit. For something he didn't know how to do. His sphere was incredible. He'd built it for victory, not to sink floating cities. It would combust if it tried to tap into the gravity beams holding up the city. Its protective chrome exterior would explode at the amount of power. If he had more time and supplies, he could probably draft up something capable of siphoning the gravity beams, but without anywhere to store the power, it wouldn't be useful.

"It's a slanting magnet!" Roman shouted to no one.

Did the sunkissers think the slummers were so stupid that they would destroy the only thing that kept the acid raid from drowning them? Roman bit against his knuckle harder. Even though he hated them and their city, he wouldn't purposely crash it on top of him.

Oliver had to know that, and he still threw Roman under the bus. Whatever Hinge had offered him to bring Roman to Icaria was going to be the first thing Roman took from Oliver. Once he got out of this cell.

Somewhere down the hallway, a door quickly opened and shut, and footsteps jogged toward him. Roman didn't bother moving, he didn't bother looking like a king. Better they think him broken before he attacked. He covered his eyes with his forearm. The residue from his Pada stuck to his eyebrows.

"Ro. Thank God you're here."

Roman was going to plan his attack. He was going to make it a show. He was going to humiliate Hinge.

He did not expect to see Oliver.

Roman torpedoed into the cell bars and grabbed Oliver by the collar of his lab coat. He pulled Oliver's face against the bars. He kept pulling, hoping the bars would slice Oliver apart. He shifted one hand and wrapped it around Oliver's throat.

"Roman." His name was a strangled breath. Oliver begged for a hundred things with that one word.

Roman denied them all. "You slanting rat."

"Ro, it's not . . ." Oliver took a gasping breath, the bars crushing his sternum. ". . . not what it looks like."

Roman laughed bitterly. "I know exactly what this is, and now you're here to gloat. Good job, Mr. Flint, you tricked an orphan boy to take the fall for your city's problem. Does it make you feel good?"

"No." Oliver reached through the bars and pushed against Roman's chest. When he didn't move, Oliver dug his nails into Roman's forearm.

Blood dripped over Oliver's nails, and Roman finally pushed him away. Oliver touched his throat, trying to rub away the red finger-shaped marks. They remained when he lowered his hand. Roman paced the cell like a monster.

"I tried telling President Hinge the truth," Oliver said, "but he wouldn't believe me. He says this is easier. Roman, why didn't you stay in the workshop? We could have figured out the gravity shortage together and fixed it. No one would have known you were here until it was safe."

As he spoke, Oliver slid his backpack off and dug into it. He strapped a pair of goggles around his forehead and handed a pair to Roman. He snatched them, wrapping them around his right fist and forming a bizarre version of a brass knuckle.

"I'm getting you out." Oliver pulled a handheld welding torch from the bag and slid his goggles over his eyes. "It's a small Byzing. Cover your eyes."

Even with his eyes shut, Roman's vision filled with the intense red light of the Byzing torch. This handheld version still had immense power. Pieces of metal crashed to the floor. When the light faded, Roman opened his eyes. Oliver had cut a hole into the bars. Oliver zipped the torch and his goggles back into the backpack and slung it over his back.

"We don't have much time. Come on, Roman."

His escape was a foot away from him, but Roman didn't move. Standing between him and freedom was a stranger inhabiting his best friend's body.

"I don't trust you."

"I don't care," Oliver said, his voice cracking with panic. He glanced down the hallway. "We have to hurry. Someone will have heard the bars breaking."

"What are you going to frame me for this time?"

"Ro, please!"

Roman crossed his arms. "Want me to build you something else before you lock me back up?"

Oliver glared at him. The expression looked terrible on him. He didn't know how to look angry. It looked too much like desperation. Too much like sadness.

"I never wanted this to happen," he blurted, his eyes darting down the hallway every few seconds. "Hinge thought you were stealing power. He thought you were planning an attack on Icaria because of how violent you are in the Ring and how your sphere appears to operate. He was going to send a whole squad of enforcers to capture you, but I offered to get you myself. I was never going to turn you in. If you and I could fix the gravity beams, then it would clear your name."

"Then why did we waste time building the Rex bot?" Roman hated that he sounded desperate and sad, too.

"Because I wanted to." Oliver reached into the cell, offering Roman his hand. "Because I wanted to be selfish and build something cool with my best friend before we had to save the city. In case things . . . Well, in case things didn't work, I wanted that time with you."

"You're not the selfish type." Roman swatted Oliver's hand away like it was an annoying fly, but he exited the cell. "I'm not going back to your house."

"No," Oliver agreed. "That's the first place they'll look. I'm getting you back to the Slums."

"How?"

"If you would shut up and move, you'd see."

"Fine." Roman stepped to the side and ushered Oliver down the hallway.

Oliver didn't take them out the way Roman expected. They jogged to the end of the hallway and stopped at a small silver door in the wall. Oliver pulled the door open to reveal a dark tunnel plummeting to nowhere. He took off his backpack and tossed it in. Roman never heard it hit the bottom.

"It's the laundry chute," Oliver explained, sticking one leg over the edge before ducking his head under the low opening. "It's the quickest way down without being seen."

Roman nodded, and Oliver pulled his other leg in and disappeared into the darkness. Roman didn't hear him hit the bottom either. He gritted his teeth. This was too convenient. This could be another one of Oliver's tricks. The main door of the hallway pushed opened, and Roman was out of time to plan his own escape. He jumped feet-first into the chute and the door shut above him, engulfing him in complete darkness.

Roman fell into a large hamper of dirty jumpsuits. The scent was the worst thing he'd smelled since being in Icaria. He climbed out of the hamper and regained his balance after falling onto the floor. Oliver threw a bundle of clothes at him.

"Put those on," Oliver ordered and turned to examine an emergency exit map nailed to the wall.

"Tell me where we are," Roman ordered back.

"Basement of Icaria Tower."

Roman examined the clothes. They looked like something he saw a guy wearing last night at the skating rink minus the white coat. He slipped out of his orange jumpsuit, tossing it behind him into the hamper, and pulled on the new clothes. He looked over Oliver's shoulder and examined the map.

"My carriage is parked here." Oliver tapped a section of the map. "Once there, I'll drive us to an elevation platform, and you'll ride it back to the Slums."

Roman adjusted the white ball cap that was included in the bundle of clothes, making it fit tighter. The symbol of Icaria, a half circle with lines extending from the top, was embroidered on the front.

"Won't someone notice a missing carriage?"

"Not my design," Oliver answered. "It's not on the market. Scrap it, melt it, keep it, do whatever you want with it once you're in the Slums."

Roman traced the map with his finger from where they were and where they needed to go. "And no one will see us getting there?"

"We'll have to be careful," Oliver answered. "You'll need to keep your head down and not say anything. We're just two employees leaving work."

Roman nodded and followed Oliver out the door, refusing to show his back to the traitor.

After walking off the sublevel elevator onto the main floor, Roman realized the building wasn't just a prison. A digital display floated in the center of the massive lobby, listing all the building's departments and their locations. There was a floor for the enforcers, for the president, for sanitation, engineering, education, new development, citizen enrichment, for anything a city needed. This building was the central hub for Icaria. The shiny beacon he'd seen when he first arrived.

Roman lowered his head as more people populated the main level and followed close behind Oliver, who had no trouble traversing the complicated layout of the corporate building. They passed under a window, and Roman felt the warm sunlight on his skin through the borrowed coat. He took a moment to stand inside the sunbeam, knowing this could be the last time he felt the sun. He chanced staring directly into it, memorizing its color, until his eyes watered. Oliver watched him carefully from a few feet away. Roman wiped away a tear and followed Oliver to the parking lot.

Oliver found his carriage among the others and unlocked the door.

"Destination?" prompted the automated voice once they were inside.

"Elevation platform," Oliver answered.

Chapter Thirteen

The window darkness remained at one hundred percent on the ride to the elevation platform. The carriage remained silent as Oliver and Roman stared at each other. Periodically, Roman would set a knuckle against his mouth, or Oliver would twist his hands together in his lap. Neither gesture lasted long, as soon as one of them realized they were being watched, their hands settled atop their knees. The ride to the platform took forever and was over too quickly. The air inside the carriage was thick.

Roman sucked in breaths through his nose, but never felt his lungs fill.

The carriage pulled into the station and settled onto a platform with a hiss.

"Ready to commence descent," the automated voice said. "Please state when ready."

Oliver tossed the backpack onto Roman's bench seat. "Everything in there is for you," he said awkwardly. "I already programmed the carriage to accept your voice controls. When you get . . ."

He trailed off. The silence angered Roman.

"Spit it out."

Oliver tapped the side of the carriage, and the door opened. He stepped out and turned back, one hand holding onto the door. He looked exactly like Liza had when Franz made her cry. His bottom lip quivered, and his green eyes were submerged in tears. Oliver was too stubborn to let them fall.

"I hope you'll forgive me," Oliver said. "If I could make things different, I would."

Failing Gravity

He closed the door before Roman could reply. Roman banged his fists against the interior of the carriage, trying to open it back up, but all he managed to do was smear blood against the wall. Whatever lock Oliver had programmed outside wouldn't operate even when Roman shouted at the computer system. The platform rumbled, lowering through the floor, and descending Roman to the Slums. Oliver's words were heavy in his head. Roman's unspoken reply sizzled on his tongue like acid.

Roman kicked the seat opposite of him. His time in Icaria was a reminder of what he didn't have. Of what Roman couldn't have. Of how easily disposable he was. He would never forgive Oliver.

He tore open the backpack and rummaged through the supplies. The Byzing hand torch and a pair of goggles were the most exciting items. The bag also contained his old clothes, some prepackaged meal replacement bars, tablets to purify water, a packet of seeds claiming to grow root vegetables in any condition, a basic tool set of the highest-grade material, and the aluminum-plated tiny robot fighter meant to be Oliver. Roman squeezed the robot until the shoulder pads bent under the pressure.

He released the robot, letting it fall back into the backpack, not having the heart to destroy it.

The last thing in the backpack was a new Pada watch that matched the one Oliver wore. The leather band looked more comfortable than the tape Roman used. By the time the carriage rumbled off the platform into the Slums, Roman had the new Pada strapped to his wrist.

All the gifts didn't distract him from his missing sphere. At least without it, he wouldn't be blamed for the continued collapse of the city. Thinking of Hinge's empire falling into a panic gave him a little joy.

"Hey robot," Roman called out. When the automated voice didn't reply, he tried again in a louder voice, "I want to set a destination!"

"Destination?" repeated the voice.

"Dead Dove."

A moment later the speakers beeped, and the voice said, "My apologies Mr. Koa, there is no destination with that name."

Roman cursed under his breath. The carriage probably needed the grid address for Dead Dove. The carriage's autopilot wouldn't have any locations programmed into its map that the sunkissers didn't need to visit. Roman powered on the display screen of his Pada, the hologram light filling the carriage. He flipped to the map application, and followed the map with his fingers from his current location to Dead Dove. Once he found it, he ordered the carriage to take him to its specific coordinates.

"Arrival time sixteen minutes," the voice said, and the carriage pulled forward down the street, unknown items crunching under its wheels.

Roman changed back into his old clothes. They smelled like daffodils. Someone had washed the T-shirt. All of the oil stains were gone. He ran his hand down the front of it. He never knew the material could become so soft under the right conditions. He stuffed the Icaria clothes into the backpack with his hat and zipped it shut.

"Hey," Roman ordered the carriage, "remove all control access except for mine."

"Request complete."

"Are there any defense modes for this thing?"

"Safety modes include: auto lock, autopilot and autopilot override, air bag deployment, and location flair. Would you like to hear more?"

"What's the location flair?"

"The location flair feature turns this carriage into a glowing orb for easy location in times of crisis."

"What makes it glow?" Roman felt around the interior of the carriage, looking for the mechanics, and found them under the bench seat across from him.

"Rerouted power from the engine alights small light sensors built into the exterior chrome body."

"What's the temperature output when that happens?"

"One hundred and six degrees."

Roman grinned. A carriage this size required a lot of power. He could easily reprogram it and have a walking bomb. Now that his sphere was gone, he needed a new bot for the Ring. Now that he was back in the Slums, he needed to do what he did best: survive. He didn't need the luxuries of Icaria. He didn't need Oliver. When Icaria crashed down, he'd have a front-row seat to the carnage.

When acid rain drenched everything, he'd go down laughing.

The carriage stopped and announced its arrival at the requested coordinates. The door popped opened. Dead Dove was in shambles across the street.

The front door was missing, a ring of ash and char circling where it had been. The windows were bashed in. Broken neon tubing littered the outside. Smoke oozed out of the roof at the back. The shipping container that had been Roman's office was dented and strips of the Corten steel were pulled back like a can opener had gnawed through it. He didn't need to look inside to know it was trashed, everything valuable taken.

Roman pocketed the Byzing torch and goggles in his jacket and programmed the carriage to lock behind him. The automated voice happily obliged and once Roman was outside, the door clicked several times activating its various locks.

The inside of Dead Dove was not any better than the exterior. The missing front door was embedded into the bar top. Whatever explosive had been used to knock it down left the front of the bar covered in soot and metal filings. Tables were overturned, chairs broken, and all of the thicker steel was gone. Neon tubing drooped from the ceiling and dropped colorful sparks on the floor. Staples sharp as sin lay on the ground and the wires they held to the walls dangled like vines. One staple embedded itself into Roman's boot as he looked behind the bar. Everything was gone.

There wasn't a drop of stardust to help swallow the loss down. Roman dug out the staple and threw it into a corner. It'd taken him almost two years to build Dead Dove. Even longer for the bar to turn a profit. It had only taken days for her to be ripped apart and gutted.

The four-pointed crown on the backdoor was crossed out by a spray-painted *X*. Roman kicked the door open and poked his head into his office. His fear was confirmed. The place was ransacked. The cabinets ripped off the wall. The TV gone. His desk sawed in half. Everything was destroyed except for the hatch on the floor. The rug hadn't been moved and Roman dropped to his knees, yanking it away and lifting the secret door.

Roman sighed. The gun he kept hidden away was still there, along with some extra ammunition. He tucked the small pistol into his waistband and closed the hatch. Maybe he'd find similar luck in the other two shipping containers.

He wasn't as lucky when he entered his workshop. The room was empty. Everything not nailed down to the floor was gone. All his unfinished projects. All his tools. Everything. He shut the door, unable to stomach the sight.

He gripped the doorknob to his living quarters and was happily surprised to find it locked. Either the thieves hadn't bothered going this far, or they were waiting inside. Either way, he'd find something good. Without his keys, he used the Byzing torch to overpower the locks, readied his pistol, and entered the shipping container. A very large part of him hoped he could shoot something.

The short hallway ahead of him was empty and dim. Neon lighting from the main room ahead didn't reach this far back. He clung to the shadows and moved forward. As he neared the main room, he heard noises to his left. Someone was in here, and they were going to regret it. Roman leapt out of the hall and aimed his gun at the intruder standing at the sink.

"Scrap?" Roman asked but didn't lower his weapon.

"Ro?" his mechanic asked, equally confused.

Scrap's mechanical arm was gone. The open socket was a mess of ripped wires. Oil dripped from it onto his shirt. His left eye was black and glossy. He had one less tooth than Roman had left him with.

"What happened?" Roman asked.

"The stardust shipment came," Scrap answered, soaking a rag in the sink's old water and pressing it against a rib under his shirt. He winced at the pressure. "But I didn't get the cryptens. I tried calling you, tried calling that sunkisser too, but the calls kept dropping. I tried to get the runners to take the dust back. I told them I'd get the scratch when you came back, but they didn't care. They took everything as payment for their wasted time. They took my slanting arm, Ro."

"They mess you up, too?" Roman asked, lowering the gun and approaching him.

"Yeah, after ripping my arm out of the socket. Roman, why the hell did you leave?"

Roman snapped back, "Why the hell did you tell them I wasn't here?"

"It slipped out."

Roman grabbed the hem of Scrap's shirt and yanked it over his chest. Dark bruises covered Scrap's rib cage, and one of the bones didn't line up with the others. Scrap forced Roman's hand away and lowered his shirt.

"I hope that job paid well," Scrap muttered, walking around Roman and collapsing in a chair across the room.

The chairs faced a window overlooking the Slums. Red and green neon flickered in the dim light. Everything looked gray and hazy. Everything looked so cold without the sun. Roman fell into the chair across from Scrap.

"The job was a scam. I should've listened to you," Roman admitted.

"Never trust a sunkisser, right? They're only good for the scrap metal they leave in the Ring. That's what you always told me."

"Yeah, I did." Oliver's and Liza's faces invaded Roman's mind. He balled his hands into fists until they faded, leaving Roman to feel like a pile of useless scrap metal. Thrown out in the Slums, again.

Scrap grumbled some more, but Roman stopped listening. When he was finished, Roman asked, "Which runner tore up Dead Dove?"

"One of Bruno's guys," Scrap answered.

"Alright." Roman pushed off the chair. "After a beer, I'm going to get my stuff back."

Roman walked to the small refrigerator under the sink and found zero beers inside.

From the couch, Scrap said, "I sort of drank them."

Roman cursed and slammed the door.

"I needed something to numb the pain," Scrap said. "You try having all your nerves ripped out your arm."

Streaks of blood stained the sink bowl. Scrap had been in more pain than just his arm.

"Where's Tansy?" Roman glanced around the room, hoping she'd materialize out of a corner.

"Crawled into her own hole to recover."

"What?" Anger caused Roman's vision to flash red. Imagining Tansy in as bad a shape as Scrap made him want to hit something. "Where?"

"Probably back home." Scrap hissed as he adjusted his position. "We put up a decent fight, but I could only protect one of them. Her or the Dove. After the runners were done with us, she left. Guess she finally got sick of looking at me. Can't be too handsome looking like this."

Scrap laughed bitterly. It was one of the few times Roman had ever seen him frown. If he hadn't been outfitted with a scrap metal prosthetic, Scrap's nickname could have been Smiles for how often he grinned. The Slums had tried to take everything from him, but it could never take that. Until now.

Until Roman let it happen by chasing his greed.

"You made the right choice," Roman said. "We'll get her back."

He'd never admit it out loud, but Roman realized in the same situation he'd let Dead Dove burn to the ground if it kept Scrap and Tansy with him.

Roman walked back to Scrap's chair and lightly kicked one of the legs. "Is my pit room the same?"

"Should be." Scrap didn't sound like he believed himself.

"Alright. Let's equip you with a new arm and then I'll get my stuff back."

Scrap looked up, blinking at him in surprise. "You have another arm lying around?"

"No, but someone has to have one."

Scrap lowered his gaze, moving the cold cloth from his ribs to his black eye. "I'm going to wait here."

"I don't have any tools here." Roman kicked the chair leg again. "Come on, I'll let you pick out the arm."

Scrap pulled himself up, groaning as the motion folded his midsection. "It's going to be the best-looking arm in there."

Roman helped him stand, then helped him to the door. "You're slanting right."

The pair left Roman's living quarters, replacing as many locks as possible with the spares Roman kept inside a drawer, and carefully traveled through the remains of Dead Dove. It still hurt Roman to see his establishment ruined. It'd take a lot of time and a lot of scratch to get it operational again. Once Scrap had two working arms and they found Tansy, he wouldn't need to do it alone.

"A carriage, really?" Scrap asked when they got outside. "This thing yours?"

"It is now." Roman tapped his Pada against the door to unlock it and they piled inside.

"Had a new Pada but couldn't message me back?" Scrap demanded, nodding at Roman's new tech.

"I was probably in jail when the delivery happened," Roman said casually. "They took my original Pada. Got this one on the way down here."

"Jail? The enforcers got you?"

Roman sighed, not wanting to relive the last few days. "Cut it. I'm back and that's all I have to say."

He'd never let Oliver and Liza cross his mind again. He was better off forgetting them.

"Destination?" prompted the automated voice. Scrap flinched at the sudden noise.

"The Ring," Roman answered.

The carriage pulled forward, and the voice said, "Arrival time eight minutes."

"How's this work?" Scrap's eyes darted around the carriage, much like Roman's had on his first trip.

"Still figuring it out," Roman answered. "But it's going to be my next bot, so don't break it."

Scrap rubbed his hand over his knee, excitement replacing his grim mood as his mechanic brain whirled with ideas. "I can't wait to tear into this thing."

Roman's chest fluttered when he opened the door to his prep room and found it exactly the way he'd left it. Even the stain of oil on the floor from Scrap's hemorrhaging project was there. Roman touched the few tools hanging on the pegboard to make sure they were real. He'd felt certain this place would be pillaged too, as the final strike before his knockout. Hope seared through his whole body before Roman could catch and squash it. Being hopeful was dangerous; getting a lucky break was almost just as bad. Both made people careless. Roman set his backpack on a clean part of the desk and set a knuckle to his teeth, thinking. The Ring was empty when they arrived, and most fighters only accessed their prep rooms the day of a fight for final adjustments, so they should be safe to roam around.

Roman turned to Scrap. "Have an arm in mind?"

"This isn't a catalog. It ain't like I can see a shopping list."

Roman rolled his eyes. Scrap had gotten really mouthy in his absence. "Fine, stay here. I'll bring one back."

Scrap followed Roman out of the room. "No, I still get my pick. Where are we starting?"

"That sunkisser's room." Franz. "Guy probably left all his spare equipment after I beat him. Wouldn't have a need for it."

"Smart thinking, Ro " Scrap caught up to him. "It would be nice to have an actual arm off a humanoid bot and not a buzz saw for a hand."

On the top floor, Roman counted off the rentable rooms the sunkissers used until he found the one that Franz had walked out of. He tried the door handle and when it didn't budge, Roman donkey-kicked it in.

The sunkisser's prep room was four times the size of Roman's and filled with luxuries he didn't have. Plush seating, a fully stocked fridge, huge monitors, drills, torches, and saws hanging from the ceiling, Roman almost drooled seeing it all. Scrap whistled beside him with the same sentiment. They were going to take a lot more than just a robot arm from this room.

"Pick one out." Roman pointed at a wall lined with three other humanoid bots. They looked like sleeping suits of armor under the gallery spotlight. Together, they probably cost a million cryptens.

Roman grabbed a crate from under a table and dumped its contents on the floor. He walked around the room, filling it like he was on a shopping spree. Roman emptied the mini-fridge of bottled waters. He took any tools that weren't in his new set off the wall. He dumped a basket of candy into the crate. He emptied a tote bag on a desk and rifled through its contents and found nothing useful except for a few copper-threaded wires. The documents inside were stamped with *Icarian High Debate Team* and *Young Leaders of Icaria Education*. Franz probably thought they made him look impressive. A sunkisser would probably believe it. Roman burned the pages to ash with a small blowtorch sitting on the table.

Taped on a wall was a blueprint for a humanoid bot that Roman assumed was the one he'd destroyed. Taped to one side of the blueprint was a list of codes that corresponded with moves on a controller. Tacked to the other side was a picture of Franz and Liza. Their arms were around each other, Liza leaning into Franz's side. They were smiling.

Roman dropped the crate. He tore the photo off the wall and ripped it to tiny pieces. They fell to the floor and Roman twisted his heel against them.

"Ro?" Scrap asked carefully across the room. "You good?"

"Fine," he growled, blowing hot air out his nose. Jealousy was harder to swallow than he remembered.

"Well, I found the one." Scrap flicked one of the robots. "Think it'll work?"

Roman picked his crate off the floor and stood beside the robot Scrap had chosen. It was a standard-looking bot. The humanoid shape was not any different from the other two beside it. The sleek black outer shell was decorated in golden swirls. Red lettering printed down the side read *Bad Ass*. Roman poked his fingers under the robot's armpit, feeling for the connections.

"It'll work."

"How do you want to get it off?" Scrap asked.

Roman grinned. He set the crate on the table behind them and removed the Byzing hand torch and goggles from his pocket. Roman snapped the goggles over his eyes and gave Scrap a two-second warning before he powered on the torch. He cut the robot's arm off at the shoulder like it was paper and stuck it inside his crate.

"Was that . . ." Scrap trailed off in disbelief, watching Roman stash the torch back in his pocket. "Is that a Byzing?"

Roman smirked. "Yeah."

"Can I use it?"

"Not a chance."

"Oh, come on, Ro!" Scrap begged, following him out of the prep room. "Please?"

Scrap begged Roman all the way back to their prep room, but Roman didn't budge. The Byzing wasn't a rusted drill bit he wouldn't lend

Scrap to use on his builds or one of the several wrenches stashed inside the workshop. All of which were now stolen and sitting in some warehouse belonging to Bruno. He'd get it all back.

And then some.

"Sit down," Roman ordered Scrap, setting the crate on a table, "and find something to bite down on."

Scrap paled slightly but did as Roman said, ripping off a strip of his shirt to shove into his mouth.

Roman cleared off the table closest to Scrap, dumped out the contents of his backpack and found the toolset. Roman pictured Oliver packing it with the tools in his workshop, the same tools they used to build their Rex Bot. He shook the image from his head. These tools were the least Oliver could have done. Roman wasn't going to feel grateful about something that was owed to him.

Using the copper wires he lifted from Franz's prep room, Roman rewrote the remaining section of Scrap's arm. This was the easy part, and Scrap sat perfectly still as Roman clipped the old wires and tethered the new ones into their proper ports. Oil stained the beds of Roman's fingernails. Once the new wires were in place, Roman retrieved the black-and-gold arm. He lined it up with the connections before lowering it on the table and adjusting a few of the ports. When he raised it up again, he locked eyes with Scrap.

The mechanic was still pale. Beads of sweat lined his hairline. His teeth sank into the T-shirt in his mouth. Roman had never had a robotic limb ripped from his torso, but he didn't doubt the pain it caused. He also didn't doubt the pain of attaching a new one.

Scrap nodded. It didn't matter if he was ready or not; he needed an arm.

Roman nodded back and set to attach each of the wires. Scrap flinched with each finished connection. He squirmed more as the minutes went by. His human hand fisted against his thigh. His eyes squeezed shut violently. After the final wire, Roman pressed the arm against the socket and used a lower-powered torch to weld the pieces together. When Roman pulled the torch away, Scrap swayed on the stool.

Roman barely caught him before Scrap fainted.

Chapter Fourteen

Roman laid Scrap across the table as gently as he could, but the dead weight of him plus the extra forty pounds of robot arm didn't make it easy. Even unconscious, Scrap winced when his arm fell against the table. His rapid breathing filled the prep room with noise, and the sweat against Scrap's face, neck, arm, everywhere left uncovered, made him glow in the lights. Pouring some bottled water onto a clean-ish rag, Roman set the cold compress over Scrap's forehead. He pulled off his coat and tossed it over Scrap as a blanket.

Scrap had acted this way when Roman attached his first arm. The fainting meant the nerves had connected, the pain short-circuiting the mechanic's brain. The fever meant the nerves were accepting the new limb, burning off any old code from the previous attachment. When they first did this, Roman had left Scrap unconscious in an abandoned shack. Scrap had found his way back to Dead Dove a few days later, ready to tend bar and do whatever else Roman told him to do as payment. This time, Roman stayed with his mechanic. He blamed Oliver and Liza for this stupid compassionate decision.

Roman cleared off the other desk, laying out his tools and spare parts he'd won in past fights. It wasn't compassion, he told himself, it was ensuring his investment survived.

But investments didn't need blankets, nor did they need a cold compress reapplied every few hours.

Roman accomplished several things while Scrap lay unconscious on his worktable. For the first time in a very long time, he slept for a full eight. According to his Pada, he reached REM twice. He added a new program to the carriage. He pillaged Franz's prep room for more parts and found a bottle of painkillers for Scrap. He also found two frozen cheeseburgers that he reheated in a microwave, leaving the greasy wrappers atop more blueprints in Franz's room as another jab at the sunkisser. He touched up his four-pointed crown on the arena floor with fresh paint. Roman also constructed a new bot from the slag of his last victory.

His sphere 2.0 sat mostly completed on a stand to keep it from rolling off the table. The outer shell was smoother than anything he'd ever felt thanks to the Byzing torch. The hatch door to the control panel fit so perfectly that Roman burned his four-pointed crown against it so he could find it in a hurry. When he held his Pada to it, the tiny door popped open and gave him access to the hollow insides where a power source still needed to be installed. Making this sphere visually different from his original, now stolen one, two horns emerged from the top. The copper-covered tips pointed toward each other with about the space of a softball between them. A gyroscopic plate underneath kept them upright and allowed the sphere to roll freely.

Roman knew it was a good build. He knew once finished, it would be the best build. He wiped his hands down the front of his pants to remove any oil and metal shavings before checking on Scrap. The mechanic had stopped shivering, and his skin had lost the clammy reptilian look it had possessed when it was covered in sweat. His breathing had balanced to something rhythmic during the last few hours. His eyes fluttered open and glanced around the ceiling, taking in the familiar lights.

Roman's chest fluttered as a weightless sensation overcame him. He stepped back from Scrap in case his mechanic would notice.

Scrap slowly sat up, and the cloth on his forehead fell into his lap with a wet smack. Roman watched with morbid curiosity as Scrap used his new hand to rub the matted hair off his forehead where it adhered to his skin. The monstrous black-and-gold arm followed Scrap's mental commands without delay. With a start, Scrap pulled the metal hand off his head and examined his new arm.

"Bad ass," he commented with a grin, curling the robotic fingers in and out of a fist.

"Works then?"

"Like a charm." Scrap stretched both arms above his head and twisted at his waist. He suddenly grabbed at his side when the pain of his broken rib overcame the thrill of his new arm.

Roman set an unopened water bottle and the bottle of pills next to Scrap. Without a word, Scrap swallowed down two pills and half the water.

"Thanks Ro."

"Whatever."

Scrap grabbed Roman's shoulder before he could choose to interact with a robot on the table instead of the human he'd fixed.

"How long have I been out?"

"A day or so."

"You stayed with me the whole time?" Scrap asked, and Roman shrugged, causing Scrap to grin wildly. "You do care about me. This arm isn't your tech, so you can't use that excuse on me this time."

"I was building a new bot." It wasn't a complete lie, but Roman still felt dirty saying it. "This is my prep room."

"You gave me your coat, too." Scrap didn't buy the lie anyway.

Roman shimmied out of Scrap's hold and pulled his jacket off him. "The sleeves got in the way of the torch. You were a coat hanger."

Even Roman didn't believe his lie. He knew the Slums would be a worse place without Scrap messing around in the Ring or at Dead Dove. Scrap was a decent slummer, and probably the only friend Roman had. He set a knuckle against his teeth.

"So, you didn't go after the stardust runners yet?"

Roman lowered his hand. "No."

"Good." Scrap slowly swung his legs over the edge of the table and stood. His right knee buckled once, but he kept his balance. "I want to give them a few licks of my own."

Roman chuckled. "Good way to test out the arm."

Scrap threw a few practice jabs with the robotic arm. Roman felt the wind off them.

"Can we still check on Tansy first?" Scrap asked.

"Think your mug is healed enough that she'll want to look at you?"

Scrap grinned, the motion sealing his still-black eye shut. "I can't see what I look like. What do you think?"

"She probably wants to give the dust runners a lick of her own, too." Roman matched Scrap's grin. "Make sure she sits on your left side though."

Roman shrugged into his coat and pocketed the Byzing hand torch. Whoever designed it probably didn't expect it to be used as a weapon, but they also probably didn't expect their sunkisser technology to find its way into the Slums.

Roman didn't have any idea where Tansy lived, but Scrap did. He rattled off the address as soon as the carriage requested their destination, and when the carriage became lost, easily directed them down different streets. Roman had assumed his mechanic and his bartender were something more than co-workers, but Scrap's intimate knowledge of her location surprised him. The carriage rumbled to the east side of the Slums. Because of weather patterns neither of them understood, most of the buildings on this side leaned to the left after being assaulted by the wind. Their wind-swept sides were corroded from acid rain and even the neon lights from Icaria couldn't fill every crevice.

Roman bit a knuckle as he wondered how badly the assault on Dead Dove had shaken Tansy for her to choose this section of the Slums to hide in when she could have stayed with Scrap inside Roman's apartment.

When the carriage stopped outside an old-world building now covered in plywood and old bicycle tires, Roman still didn't have an answer. When they approached the door, Scrap used his human hand to knock twice, pause, then knock four more times. Roman didn't recognize the code. He didn't know how long they'd been using it. He didn't know why the secret felt like a betrayal.

The door pulled open slightly, and half of Tansy's face appeared in the gap. She gasped and slammed the door, yanking the various chain locks off before throwing it open. She looked better than Scrap when Roman found him, but not by much. A sock was taped to the side of her face, hiding an injury under her eye, and strips of cloth were wrapped around her arms. Some were clean, others were still damp and red.

Tansy threw her arms around Scrap and squeezed, making them both flinch, but Scrap welcomed her touch with a goofy grin. As she left his embrace, Roman tensed, expecting her to welcome him the same way.

Her fist slammed into his chest instead.

"You never should have left," she spat. Her bandaged wounds looked more like a warning than a vulnerability. "This happened because you went star-chasing with a damn sunkisser. You should have paid the runners in advance. Or if you were going to abandon us, a heads up would have been nice. Scrap and I were sitting ducks while you were doing who knows what up there."

"I know," Roman said. "I'm sorry."

Tansy's rage deflated. Scrap blinked owlishly at him. Roman repeated himself, unsure if even he heard his apology.

"You're right, Tansy," he continued. "I should've given you the cryptens before I left, but I wasn't abandoning either of you, or the Slums. I was always coming back."

Tansy crossed her arms. "Why didn't you send the money?"

"I was arrested. They took my Pada."

"Seems convenient," Tansy replied.

"Roman was played," Scrap added.

"What happened up there?" she asked.

Roman shook his head. "I'll tell you, both of you, but not here. Not now." Not when the Flints haunted his vision whenever he closed his eyes. "We need to get the Dove back. I need to go see Bruno."

Tansy tensed at the dust runner's name. "I won't go there."

Roman continued to surprise himself with compassion. "I won't make you. I wanted to bring Scrap here, so he'd quit whining about you."

Scrap shrugged, not refuting Roman. "I wanted to make sure you were okay. Now that my arm's back, I can protect you again."

Tansy set her hand against the black metal of Scrap's robot arm before sliding it up and resting it against his cheek. "Thank you."

Scrap's face turned the same shade as the red neon lights, burning bright in the night. Tansy faced Roman, and he shifted his weight in case she was going to throw another punch, or worse.

"I'll meet you at the Dove," she said. "I'll gather what I can on my way over. Be careful."

"I will," Roman replied, his insides feeling light and uncomfortable again.

"I was talking to Scrap."

Roman grinned at her. This was the Tansy he'd hired. She was beautiful in a brass knuckle kind of way. A fighter. Not a mother hen to fuss over him. Silently, as he watched Tansy and Scrap exchange a quick goodbye, he realized they were his family. In ways he was completely unprepared for, his mechanic and bartender had filled the holes that the Flints had left, that the death of his mother had left, that he had left in himself.

"Tansy," Roman said as Scrap headed back to the carriage, "I do think your tattoos are cool."

"I know," she said. "You be careful too, Ro."

Roman stared at her, allowing the fluttering in his stomach to pass, and then he gave her the pistol he had tucked into the waistband of his pants. She accepted the gun, checked the magazine and counted the ammunition before tucking it behind her back. It was as intimate a goodbye as Roman could give, but it still left him exposed and he was almost okay with the feeling.

Chapter Fifteen

Roman didn't bother kicking over any of the hornet's nests that belonged to the smaller stardust distillers. It would have taken a skilled crew to tear apart Dead Dove the way she was, so Roman went straight to the top. The owner and operator of the whole stardust operation: Bruno Mickyvillie. Even if his stuff wasn't with Bruno, the man would know which of his employees had it.

Roman and Scrap rode the carriage to the far edge of the Slums. The automated voice informed them several times that there was no street to continue down, and Roman barked an override code forcing the carriage to continue. The carriage bucked as it wheeled across mounds of trash and dipped into small trenches caused by acid rain blowing in. Roman lowered the window darkness to fifty percent, but the areas near the edge were so hazy with corrosive weather he could hardly see out the window. Flashes of blue light from some nearby gravity station peppered the sky before darkness devoured it.

He parked the carriage a street away from the warehouse. Roman had informed Scrap of their battle plan, and the kid was ready for a fight. Roman wasn't sure it would come down to one. Bruno wasn't known for his compassion, but he was for upholding his deals. The inside of Roman's throat burned from breathing in the acid-concentrated air. He flipped up the collar of his jacket, and Scrap did the same. Ahead of them, outside the protection of Icaria, silver rain crashed to the ground. It was a curtain of death. Bruno's warehouse sat ten yards away from it, the backside smoldering and steaming from the acid. It was either a show of power or insanity. Sometimes Roman thought they were the same thing.

Roman pulled his goggles over his forehead and banged against the front door. When it opened slightly, Roman inserted the hand torch and pulled the trigger, shutting his eyes against the light. The crack between the door and wall lit up cherry-red and whoever stood behind it screamed. Roman released the switch and kicked the door in. It slammed into Bruno's goon, who collapsed against a wall, and Roman held the torch like a gun and entered the warehouse.

Just because Bruno could be civil didn't mean his goons would be. Breathing in the raw stardust fumes for too long melted their brains.

Thick wires hung from the low ceiling like vines connecting various containers to a big vat in the back. The room stank of rotten food and something acrid. Small fires burned in trash cans every couple of meters adding an unintentional smoke screen. Roman and Scrap stood at the top of a long table which split the room in half. The stardust distillers, wearing ripped plastic ponchos and thick rubber gloves, turned to them. They didn't look too imposing, but they outnumbered Roman and Scrap significantly. It was no wonder they overtook Dead Dove.

The closest distiller ran for Scrap while the farthest one inched away from the table. Scrap punched the distiller's nose with his robot hand and the man dropped to the ground, his body disappearing in the smoke. The rest of the distillers scattered like rats, some moving toward Scrap to take a shot at him and the rest running deeper into the warehouse.

Glass containers of stardust shattered, and metal tables dented under the weight of bodies as Scrap tossed the runners in every direction. Knowing Scrap had this situation under control, Roman ran after the others, hoping they would lead him to Bruno, who he suspected was lounging in a back room somewhere. Roman fired off spouts of Byzing fire as he rounded corners and crossed under catwalks stretching above the vats. The heat was enough to keep people off him, but it also began blistering his finger managing the trigger.

Ahead of him, one distiller ran into a room and Roman quickly followed, kicking the door in, and blasting the interior with a shower of fire. When the blinding light vanished, Roman opened his eyes and sneered at Bruno. The man ate well for a slummer. His belly bulge slipped out of his ratty T-shirt. A pair of glasses held his greasy, slicked-back hair in place, showing off the liver-colored birth mark on his forehead. He stood in the center of a room filled with oddities. Mounds of rubber tires, upturned tables with broken legs, several stacks of old-world metal street signs, a pile of robot parts that would make a junkyard dog drool. Roman found his Dead Dove sign sitting among them.

"Roman." Bruno tossed the pad of paper he held to the ground and crossed his arms, his eyes watering from the Byzing's light.

"Bruno." Roman kept his finger on the trigger. His plan to handle this civilly evaporated as the dust runner stared him down. The damage to his eyes from the Byzing didn't make Bruno look vulnerable. It had the opposite effect: red daggers aimed straight for Roman's throat.

"Been wondering where you were hiding."

"You destroyed my bar."

"Your boy didn't have my payment."

Bruno stepped to the left, and Roman tracked his movement. They circled each other like wild animals. Roman scanned the area in front of him, looking for things Bruno could easily grab and use as a weapon. The most dangerous option was the broken slabs of wood. They would give Bruno enough reach to bash in Roman's skull, but an easy thing for the torch to burn through. Roman wasn't scared.

"Then you should've taken back your stardust," Roman growled. "Now you owe me for my whole Dove."

Bruno laughed. "Call it interest, call it collateral, call it whatever you want, but you know that's how to run a business."

"Thought you were better than a thief."

Dead Dove was tiny compared to the size of Bruno's stardust operation, but Roman wouldn't tarnish his bar's name with the kind of business tactics Bruno employed. Roman may have gotten everything through blood, but he was always willing to spill his too.

As Roman turned, he saw another pile of junk against the back wall, and his breath hitched. Oliver knelt amongst the trash. A dingy gag was stuffed in his mouth, and his arms were pinned behind him with leftover distilling tubes. His bright eyes were as dim and hazy as the fog outside, and their haunted look cut Roman to his core. Roman couldn't look away from the bruises blossoming on Oliver's arms and neck, from the dried blood under his ear, from Oliver's bare feet smeared with grime. Roman squeezed his eyes together, hoping to remove the ghost, but Oliver remained. Oliver was here, kidnapped in a Slum warehouse. He tried to say something, but the gag muffled his warning.

A chunk of wood slammed against Roman's shoulder, and he howled in pain. Bruno wielded the wood like a bat and smashed it into Roman's shoulder a second time, and a third before Roman could slip out of range. He pulled the trigger on the torch and turned the wood to char, burning Bruno's hand in the process. It didn't stop him however, and before Roman could ready his next attack, Bruno whacked the metal Dead Dove against Roman's face, knocking him to the ground.

Roman wiped the back of his hand across his cheek and cleared the blood oozing from the new cut. Bruno circled him. His mouth moved but Roman couldn't hear anything over a metallic ringing in his ears. He slowly pushed himself up, pretending one of his legs had given out. Bruno laughed at his weakness.

Roman's hearing came back in time to hear Bruno's final insult.

"... you'll never be a king, you filthy slanting rat."

Roman leapt forward and stuck the still-hot torch end under Bruno's chin, gripping his other hand around the back of Bruno's neck. When the man tried to jerk away, Roman pushed harder into his bottom jaw. The smell of burning flesh replaced the rotten citrus stench of the stardust.

The torch was off, but all Roman saw was red. Anger burned through him hot enough to be viewed from space. This thief had stolen his bar, hurt his friends, and now taken Oliver. Roman almost pulled the torch's trigger, but this close the Byzing would burn him too.

"I'm taking my stuff back," Roman said.

"I already sold most of it," Bruno whimpered against the torch. A bright red spot formed against it from the residual heat; blisters popped and bubbled on his skin.

From the corner of his eye, Roman watched Bruno's hand slowly reach toward him. Roman pressed lightly against the Byzing's trigger, and the metal end heated preparing for a full blast. Roman leaned closer to Bruno and dared him to move again. Roman looked like the wild animal everyone imagined he was. Even he wasn't sure if he'd rip out Bruno's throat with his teeth or use the torch to finish the job. When Bruno lowered his hand, Roman released the trigger.

"Give me the credits." Roman kicked Bruno's boot. "Now."

Roman stepped back, fearing he might kill the man before he got his scratch, but kept the torch aimed at Bruno's face as he programmed the transfer. Roman's Pada dinged happily when the new cryptens landed in his account. He stepped back toward Oliver and told him to stand, yanking the old tubing away from the wall.

"Hey!" Bruno shouted. The man turned rigid when Roman trained the Byzing torch back at his face. "I didn't take that boy from Dead Dove."

"I said I'm taking back what's mine," Roman said. "Doesn't matter where you got it."

Roman tried pulling the gag away from Oliver's mouth, but Oliver shook his head and kept mumbling into it. Oliver thrashed against the tubes around his wrists and knocked his shoulder into Roman's nose.

"Cut it!" Roman barked at him. "I'm trying to—"

A pair of burned hands violently pulled Roman away, throwing him across the room. He landed on his back, the impact stealing his breath. Bruno glared down at Roman, his eyes bulbous and blood shot. This was the side of Bruno's power that was insanity. Roman eyed the Byzing torch that had been knocked from his hands, now laying across the room. He returned to his feet despite the protest in his lungs. Roman feinted right then ran to the left to grab the Byzing, but Bruno was too fast. He knocked Roman to the ground and kicked relentlessly at his ribs.

Roman grabbed onto Bruno's other leg and bit his calf hard. Roman didn't let go until blood welled in his mouth, but Bruno didn't stop.

"Stop it!" Oliver's voice pierced the carnage.

Suddenly, Bruno's assault stopped, and his massive body slumped to the ground. Roman rolled away, pressing against his wounded side as he returned to his feet. Roman spat blood, a mixture of his and Bruno's, on the ground. He looked at Oliver who loomed over Bruno's body, a metal rod in his hands. Blood dripped from it onto the dirty floor.

"O?" Roman asked, forcing Oliver to look away from Bruno. Oliver's hands tightened against the rod and Roman walked to him, slowly placing his hands over Oliver's and pushing the rod down. "You're okay."

"Roman I . . ." Oliver kept glancing from Roman to Bruno, and then to his hands slick with the blood running down the rod.

"You saved my life," Roman finished for his friend. "Besides, the bastard's not dead, just unconscious."

"He is?" Oliver's attention snapped back to Roman. Relief painted his face as clearly as the blood did his hands.

"Yeah." Roman didn't bother checking how truthful his statement really was. "Let's get out of here before that changes and he wakes up."

Oliver dropped the rod, and Roman kicked it away from them. Oliver looked ready to collapse. Now that he wasn't in a fight, Roman saw the dark circles around his eyes and how some of the blood on the side of his head was still fresh. Somewhere beneath all his curly hair was a cut that needed fixing. It would have to wait though. Roman retrieved his Byzing and led them out of Bruno's backroom. Inside the main distilling room, Scrap waited by the door. He gave Oliver a nasty look but didn't question Roman as he ordered them to move. Scrap fell in line and watched Roman's back until they made it to the carriage. None of them let out a proper breath until they were inside and the door locked.

"What the slant are you doing here?" Roman barked as Oliver untied the gag that had slid around his neck during the fight.

Oliver ran the back of his hand across his mouth. The corners of his lips were acid burnt, tiny and angry blisters erupting from his skin. "Some guy grabbed me as soon as I landed and dragged me here."

"I meant the Slums." Roman's demeanor was still hostile at best.

"I was exiled."

Scrap whistled. "Serves a sunkisser right."

Roman slapped the back of his hand into Scrap's bruised side and caused the mechanic to wheeze. "What do you mean 'exiled'?"

Oliver tried to mirror Roman's hostility but sounded more like an upset child than angry king. "It wasn't hard for Hinge to figure out who freed you."

"I never asked you to do that!"

"You didn't need to, Ro!" Oliver's outburst seemed to surprise him, but he let it carry him. "You're my best friend. I would've done anything to save you. That's why I brought you up there. It's why I was trying to hide you from Hinge in the first place!"

"Why didn't Hinge just kill you then?" Roman fired right back, Oliver's compassion like a whip against his skin. "For breaking all the rules for a slummer."

"Said it'd be too easy." Oliver crossed his arms. "Apparently, a death sentence was too generous when I could be sent here."

"You'd probably want the death sentence depending on what Bruno had in store for you," Scrap said, and flinched when Roman glared at him, but Roman kept his hands to himself, biting a knuckle until it bled.

"You weren't there to save me, were you?" Oliver asked, sounding more like himself.

"No," Roman answered. "But I wasn't going to let him keep you."

"Thank you," Oliver said, then turned to Scrap. "Thank you, too."

When Roman didn't respond, Scrap asked, "What do we do now, boss?"

This, Roman did know. "We secure the Dove and get her operational again."

"And Icaria?" Oliver asked.

Roman lowered his hand and looked out the window. The hazy fog of the outskirts gave way to the usual dimness of neon lights and shadows. "Now that you're here," he told Oliver, "you're better off forgetting that place."

"But the gravity—"

"It's their problem," Roman interrupted coldly. He couldn't do anything to fix the problem down here. It was Icaria's mess and the sunkissers would have to solve it. It didn't matter anymore.

Roman programmed the carriage to stop at a shoddy house made of old dog houses stacked on top of each other. The various oval doors created a beehive effect, and the building stretched high above them. Roman purchased a few pieces of metal roofing and the least-rusted nails they had for sale. The price was more than he wanted to pay, but the convenience of not digging through the dumps softened the financial blow. Once Dead Dove was open again, he'd make back his cryptens. He added a few three-legged bar stools to his tab and had Scrap tie everything to the roof of the carriage.

Tansy waited for them at Dead Dove, waving as the carriage neared. She'd replaced her bandages for thicker gauze and tape and removed the patch from her face completely. Both her smile and the curved cut under her eye greeted them. She lowered a duffle bag off her shoulder as Roman approached.

"Found what I could." she nudged the bag with her boot, "but you didn't give me a lot of time."

"Bruno was smart enough not to waste my time," Roman replied. "Told him you said hi, by the way."

Tansy scoffed. "It better have been with your fist."

"A Byzing torch, actually."

In Tansy's stunned silence, Roman knelt and examined what she had found. Between the two of them, their supplies were limited, but being a slummer meant you survived with and without. "Start with the fryers," he told her. "I don't want any grease explosions."

"Not that the place could get much worse," Tansy said, but retreated inside the bar to get started.

Fixing the outside of Dead Dove was easy, especially with Scrap's new arm. The mechanic held up the metal sheets as if they were bedsheets while Roman patched them to the exterior walls using the Byzing hand torch. Its bright red light drew a crowd, but the slummers were as useless as the moths they acted like. Roman had half of the front exterior fixed when someone tugged at the back of his shirt.

"What?" Roman demanded, turning around ready for a fight.

The small boy that he'd let pick up trash the other night flinched, but offered a handful of nails to Roman. "I picked these up last time, can they work?"

Roman's cheeks flushed in the Byzing's heat, and he lowered the torch. "Not for this," he told the kid, "but you can go about fixing that window frame. Can you use a hammer?"

The boy nodded.

"We don't have one, so see what you can scrounge up and use that, got it?"

The boy nodded again and took off, kicking around in garbage piles until he found a good-size rock to use as a hammer.

Scrap grinned at Roman like he'd just heard the best joke of his life. "Seems like you've got another one."

Roman glanced over his shoulder as another man approached them. Roman recognized him by his usual order, two beers and a plate of fried mushrooms, but didn't know his name. He held a milk crate full of tools and strips of wire.

"Your power box is sparking," he told Roman. "I can patch it up for you."

"What's your charge?" Roman asked. He could patch the power box himself, but it would save time hiring it out.

"We can wash my tab?" the man suggested. "I know I've gotten away with a few free beers."

Roman glared at Scrap who suddenly needed to reinspect their last welding job. "Fine," he told the man.

Roman told Scrap to finish the walls and stepped back to examine Dead Dove. The same fluttering feeling overcame him as he watched strangers offer to help restore his bar. People he just saw as easy cryptens rolled up their sleeves and got their hands dirty. For him. Roman helped the boy hold the window frame as he pounded a nail in.

Restoring the inside of Dead Dove was not as easy as the exterior.

"Get all the glass and junk off the floor," Roman ordered Scrap and handed him a broom. Scrap nodded and set to work, easily lifting tables out of the way with his new arm. Roman pointed at the bar and looked at Oliver. "Find a bucket and sponge and clean the walls. The paint ought to come off with a little stardust in the water."

Oliver looked around Dead Dove, absorbing the weight of the task with a groan. Graffiti covered the walls. Obscenities screamed at him, overpowering the four-pointed crowns and sparrow silhouettes etched underneath.

"This could take a while," Oliver said.

"Then you better get started." Roman said.

"What are you going to do?"

Roman glared at him, but answered, "Fix the lighting."

Seeming to accept his answer, Oliver headed to the bar to find what little cleaning supplies Dead Dove contained.

Roman collected the better-looking neon tubing off the walls and ceiling and brought it to his workshop. He swapped his Byzing for a solder and began his repairs.

With the neon lights fixed, his bloody knuckles patched up, and the Byzing torch charging, Roman exited his workshop and actually smiled. His Dove was taking shape. Scrap had salvaged a few tables and was bending a forgotten pipe into a fourth leg for one of them. Tansy had managed to get the bar back in order and was ready to serve a drink if they could find any glasses. One of the walls was scrubbed clean and the carving of a sparrow wearing his crown shined against the newly-polished siding. He made a mental note to add a peppering of stars that would match Tansy's tattoo to the empty space. And something for Scrap. A couple of gears to match the ones rotating in his head. Roman affixed the lights along the walls and the room glowed with color again.

Scrap finished securing the table leg, stood up, and dusted off his hands. "Looking good, right?"

Roman nodded. "Looking real good."

Scrap beamed at the compliment. "What's next on the list?"

"Help Tansy stock the bar," Roman answered. "We'll use the stuff in my place for now."

"I think I drank most of it."

Roman fought the urge to lash out at him. Knowing Scrap had found a little comfort after the attack was worth more than the little scratch he'd get for selling a few beers. "There's more in the bedroom. Bottom of the dresser."

"Got it, boss."

"Scrap?" Roman called before his mechanic got too far away. Scrap turned around and waited for his demand. "One free drink."

Scrap chuckled. "I never thought I'd see the day. Thanks, Ro."

Roman waited for Scrap to get distracted by Tansy before approaching Oliver. He was scrubbing at the wall with such vigor his nail beds had started to bleed. When he dunked his rag into his coffee can of cleaner, he winced but didn't stop. Roman kneeled next to him, wet his own rag, and scrubbed alongside him. They cleaned away half of the phrase *death to the king* before Roman asked, "How's the Rex Bot?"

Oliver smiled slightly. "Safe in my workshop."

"Should've brought it with you," Roman half joked. "That beast belongs in the Ring."

"Think anything could stand a chance against it?"

"Not unless we built it."

They both laughed, Roman's a sharp and jagged bark and Oliver's a happy chuckle. The noises clashed, but the owners somehow fit side by side.

"Your mouth hurt?" Roman asked after silence engulfed them.

Oliver kept scrubbing. "A little."

"I've got something that'll help," Roman admitted, the simple kindness sounding like a secret. "I'll get it for you tonight. Acid burns are the worst."

"I didn't think I got close enough to the edge to get rained on," Oliver said.

"It was in the gag." Roman soaked his rag. "Seen it before with Bruno."

"Charming guy." Oliver gritted his teeth, scrubbing the wall harder.

Roman pushed Oliver's hands down, forcing him to look at him. "No one will mess with you now. Work the Dove and stay with me. I'll protect you."

"I can't stay here."

Roman looked like he'd been slapped. Anger boiled up his throat. "This place not good enough for you?" *Am I still not good enough?*

"I have to get back to Icaria."

Roman dunked his rag and scrubbed halfheartedly. "Thought you were exiled."

"Liza's still there. I won't leave her."

"You can't bring her down here," Roman barked, then added more civilly, "She'll get sick again."

Oliver attacked the wall with his rag. "Don't you think I know that?"

Roman was sure Oliver had thought of everything. He was sure he'd run through every scenario that could get him back to Icaria. He was sure Oliver had tweaked every plan and accounted for every step that could go wrong. Roman was certain Oliver had forgotten one thing, however.

"I built a new bot," Roman said slowly.

"Now's not the time, Ro," Oliver scolded.

"It slanting is." Roman's smile was as crooked as his painted crown on the wall. "You're only getting up there if you do something to impress Hinge. That guy thought I built something to drain the grav stations, so I did one better. My new bot can power them. Keep your dumb city floating."

Oliver's eyes widened. The rag fell into the coffee can with a splash.

Chapter Sixteen

Holding his sphere 2.0, Roman kicked open his prep room door. Mr. O'Neal stood in the hallway, the door missing him by a few inches. Roman and the announcer blinked, neither expecting to find company this late in the night. Roman's teeth clamped together, and he readied his sphere to use as a blunt weapon in case Mr. O'Neal had come to take him away for stealing Franz's stuff. By the law of the Slums, it was technically Roman's for beating him. By the law of Icaria, the sunkisser could spend however many crytpens he wanted to get it back and toss Roman back in jail, or out into the wastelands.

"Oliver Flint!" Mr. O'Neal exclaimed, looking past Roman into his prep room where Oliver stood. "What a sight for these old eyes. O and Ro back at it again, are you?"

Oliver shoved past Roman and wrapped the old man in a hug. "Mr. O'Neal!" Oliver released him. "I didn't think I'd see you here. There's not a fight tonight, is there?"

"Not till the weekend."

Roman exhaled. He needed a quiet night for his plan to work. He knew the Ring's fight night schedule, but Mr. O'Neal lurking outside his prep room made him question a lot of things. Like what was the announcer doing outside his lavish home when he didn't need to be? His status as a wealthy slummer painted as big a target on his back as if he were a sunkisser.

"What are you doing here?" Roman asked, interrupting Oliver's polite conversation.

Mr. O'Neal didn't seem bothered by Roman's rudeness. He pointed a thumb over his shoulder at a dolly stacked with cardboard boxes.

Dark grease spots covered most of them. "Wanted to drop these off for you."

Roman rose on his tiptoes to see inside the box, but he was too far away to get a decent look. "What's in it?"

"Stuff for Dead Dove," Mr. O'Neal answered. "I heard what happened. A friend of mine saw you rebuilding. He wanted to donate these old things to the cause."

"What's in it?" Roman asked again, his patience dwindling.

Oliver frowned. "Whatever it is, you can use it." Oliver addressed Mr. O'Neal, "Ro lost everything in that bar. Tell your friend thanks, this is really nice."

Mr. O'Neal nodded to Oliver. "I was just going to stick it in here for Roman to find later. Figured that'd be for the best."

Oliver chuckled. "He never learned how to accept a gift."

Roman grumbled, holding open the prep room door so Mr. O'Neal could wheel the dolly inside. "You don't get anything here for free." He was still budgeting how much the charity work from the little boy and electrical worker were going to cost him.

"Well, these are on me." Mr. O'Neal parked the dolly and looked around the prep room before setting his gaze back on the boys. Their clothes were stained with oil. Oliver had tucked a pencil behind his ear. Roman's hair was a frenzied mess tangled within the goggles on his head. The prep room smelled of machinery. "You boys really are back." Mr. O'Neal smiled. "Building something?"

"Just the final touches on Roman's bot," Oliver replied proudly, setting his hand on the top of sphere 2.0.

"I look forward to seeing it in action." Mr. O'Neal exited the prep room, chuckling as he walked down the hallway toward the exit. "I look forward to seeing more of the two of you together. O and Ro, back again."

Roman grumbled. The old man was becoming delusional in his old age, thinking he and Oliver were back building robots again. Their Rex bot had been a one-time thing. After Roman saved Icaria, he wouldn't see Oliver again. He swallowed down the fact and it caught in his throat. "We need to go."

Oliver sighed, interlocking his hands behind his head. "O and Ro, back again," he repeated. "Could be fun, don't you think?"

Roman thought it could be a lot of things. Fun was on the list, but so was hope and that was a useless emotion. It sat right next to betrayal. He walked ahead with his sphere. "Won't be any point in fighting if your city crashes down."

Outside the Ring, the air hummed with electricity. Now that Roman had seen the failing gravity station, he couldn't ignore the lightning strikes dancing in the distance. Bile thick as rain burned the back of his throat. If Icaria couldn't fix the problem, would they have warned the Slums? Given the people a chance to flee before their city flattened this place? Roman spat on the ground, knowing the answer. Of course, Hinge wouldn't. Oliver and Liza were the best people up there, and they had come from the Slums.

"Ro," Oliver called from inside the carriage, "you good?"

Roman tore his eyes off the newest lightning strike that painted the underside of Icaria in a spiderweb of light and climbed in.

Once Roman ordered the carriage to take them to the elevation platform, he repacked his backpack with his tools and fit sphere 2.0 safely inside. He changed the order of the wrenches several unnecessary times. Mr. O'Neal's voice kept whirling inside his head. Oliver's hope made his stomach churn. *O and Ro back again.* Roman zipped his pack and set a knuckle to his mouth. That could never happen. The Slums was no place for the Flints now.

"What type of power source do you need for the new sphere?" Oliver asked, his thoughtful eyes never leaving Roman.

"Bigger the better," Roman answered. "Where is the main hub for the gravity stations?"

"Each beam goes to its own cap under the disk."

"There's not a master control somewhere?"

Oliver frowned. "There is. It's inside the Icaria Department of Science and Technology."

Roman blinked at him.

"The place I broke you out of," Oliver explained. "Icaria Tower. Well, same building but different level. Everything that happens in Icaria is controlled and monitored there."

"You'll need to get me in."

"We're both fugitives," Oliver reminded. "I don't even know how to get back into Icaria. The guards at the elevation platform won't let me pass."

Roman grinned wickedly. "I've got that taken care of."

"I don't like the sound of that at all." Oliver's chuckle didn't make Roman believe him. It was the same laugh Roman heard growing up when he dumped a bunch of scrap at Oliver's feet and told him about his plans for it. Oliver would tell him it wouldn't work, then the two of them would spend all night getting it as close to Roman's wicked idea as they could.

"Computer," Roman barked at the carriage. "Window darkness one hundred percent."

After the windows darkened, a soft glow of light illuminated the carriage as small overhead track lights turned on.

"Computer, change user status to Franz Eddison."

"It can't do that," Oliver protested.

"Change complete," the computer responded.

Oliver cocked an eyebrow at Roman, and Roman shrugged. "I had time to reprogram your carriage."

"What else did you do?" Oliver asked, and Roman thought he saw a glimmer of his own wicked smile behind Oliver's eyes. It was a hunger that could only be fed by tearing apart machinery and rebuilding it into something of your own.

The carriage slowed to a stop, and someone outside knocked against the hull. The person called in a groggy voice for their identification.

Roman said to Oliver in a hushed voice, "Icaria guards thin out at night. Most sunkissers that elevate this late are sleeping, your dumb carriages taking them back on autopilot."

"This can't work." Oliver sank against his bench seat, his legs slipping onto the floor, so not to be seen through the blacked-out windows.

The guard outside knocked again and when neither of them answered, the carriage beeped as he scanned the Pada code. Franz would pop up as the owner. When the carriage rumbled forward, Roman knew his plan was working. After a few minutes the carriage started rising. Oliver straightened in his seat, and Roman waited for him to rescind his doubt.

Oliver never did.

If his device didn't work, then his home would be destroyed. His friends would be too. Oliver's doubt seeped into him. Roman shouldered his backpack when the carriage signaled their arrival in Icaria. The straps pulled against his back with the weight of his sphere and made his midsection pulse from Bruno's assault. He relished in the pain and let it ground him. Roman needed to focus. He didn't have time for foolish things like hope and doubt.

Examining his Pada, Oliver announced, "We're approaching the decontamination center."

Roman looked at the ceiling. The F for Flint looked back at him. "Computer, commence operation Big Bang in five minutes."

"What's operation 'Big Bang'?" Oliver asked.

"Operation Big Bang commencing in five minutes," responded the computer.

"Do you want to stay around and find out?" Roman asked.

"No, I guess I don't," Oliver replied. "But, Ro, what's our plan for getting out of here?"

"On my signal, run like hell."

When the carriage stopped inside the decontamination center, Roman lessened the window darkness by fifteen percent to check their surroundings. The room was empty, just as it had been when he first arrived in Icaria. He slowly exited the carriage and peered around the room to make sure they were alone. The glass box that had blasted him with clean and scented air looked like a jail cell. He felt better knowing it wouldn't be in one piece much longer. Roman checked the time. His five minutes were almost up. He bumped his fist against Oliver's shoulder to get his attention and led him away from the carriage. Roman kicked over a metal table, and they both crouched behind it.

"I'm not going to like this operation, am I?" Oliver asked, covering the top of his head with both arms.

"Probably not." Roman mirrored his protective stance. "You said you made other carriages, right?"

"Just the blueprints."

"You can make more."

The room erupted in light and sound as the carriage exploded. Parts of it slammed against the table, denting their makeshift shield. The floor rumbled. Pieces of the ceiling collapsed above the carriage. The glass box shattered. Cool air snuck in through the broken walls. A few sections were missing completely. The carriage was reduced to ash and a few melted wheels. Somewhere outside, the wailing of enforcer carriages pierced the night.

"You brought them right to us!" Oliver shouted in a panic.

"Yeah, but we aren't staying." Roman tugged Oliver to his feet. "Get up. We have to move. Now!"

Through a jagged hole barely big enough to fit one person, Roman and Oliver tumbled out of the decontamination center into an alley behind the building. Dust and ash from the explosion helped cover their escape as they ran from the remains of the building and the screeching tires of the Icaria Enforcers. When they were several streets away, Oliver took the lead and the pair slowly traveled to the center of the city, clinging to the shadows.

The dust didn't dissipate the farther they got from the explosion. Roman realized his throat wasn't burning just from the exertion of running. The way each swallow felt like a blade down his throat was both unwanted and familiar. When Oliver paused behind a dumpster to catch his breath, Roman kicked at the dust. It was thick and didn't cling to his boot like it should. He swiped his fingers through the inch-deep substance and hissed at the pain it caused his still-healing knuckles.

"It started happening a day or two before I was exiled," Oliver explained. "Wasn't this far into the city, though; just around the edge of the park."

"It's acid fog." Roman straightened, wiping his hand against his shirt. He pictured the tiny acid waves that lapped against Icaria's edge leaking across the park and burning the flowers and grass. "Icaria has already started sinking below the clouds."

"We have to hurry."

Roman nodded. "Get us into the tower."

Oliver consulted his Pada a final time before looking up at Icaria Tower looming high above them. Its upper floors glowed a fuzzy yellow with interior lights. Oliver probably walked to that tower every day. He probably used his Pada to enter the front door like a civilian. He probably knew the layout of the building so well because he worked there. He was probably respected there.

"I know you can get us in." Roman touched Oliver's shoulder and quickly lowered his hand. "Let's fix the gravs so your life can get back to normal."

Oliver swallowed, but his voice sounded more chipper than before. "Thought you hated Icaria. Why go to the trouble of saving it?"

Roman gritted his teeth. "It's worth the trouble for you. Now, get me in there before I change my mind."

"Okay." Oliver's smile was triumphant and annoying. It reminded Roman of the sun so much that he couldn't look at it. "It's a good thing we grew up crawling through the trash, because the dumpster chute will be the best way in."

They hung on the sleek sides of buildings, crouched behind wide flowerpots and trees, hopped from shadow to shadow, froze at every footstep and siren. Red lights bathed the city as the enforcers searched for the person responsible for the explosion. The frantic search kept them busy, but their chaotic movement forced Oliver to lead Roman in a zig zag to the tower. What should have taken ten minutes took a full half hour.

Oliver interlaced his fingers to give Roman a boost into the metal opening a few feet above them. The air drifting out of the trash chute was humid and smelled of home: old food and grime. It actually comforted Roman. He almost expected the sunkissers to clean their trash so nothing would be imperfect in their golden city.

Roman stepped onto Oliver's hands and leapt into the chute, using his forearms to brace himself on either side and shimmied forward onto a more leveled section. He awkwardly turned around and offered Oliver his hand. It was a struggle to get them both into the trash chute, but once inside, they scurried down the metal tunnel like rats. Oliver offered directions from the back as they came to turns and forks in the chute. Roman kept his body pressed low against the chute so his sphere wouldn't drag against the top.

"Our exit's on the left," Oliver announced.

"Finally," Roman grunted, gaining speed once he knew he'd be out of the tunnel soon. His chin scraped along the metal in his haste, and he punched through the first vent cover on his left, tumbling onto the ground with a huff.

The hallway looked the same as the one outside his cell. White walls, white tile floor, bright lights on the ceiling that made Roman look like a dark smear. He wiped his grimy boots against the floor to leave a disgusting boot print.

"We need to hurry," Oliver said, straightening his coat as he stood. "There's a stairwell down the hall. The gravity power room is still a few floors up."

"Then why'd we get out here?"

"I couldn't handle the smell," Oliver answered.

Roman shook his head but didn't protest. He was glad not to be cramped up anymore. He ran down the hall and took the stairs two at a time, ascending to the door marked with a large eight. Roman yanked it open.

A lone figure stood in this hallway, his eyes shifting from surprise to anger as they narrowed on Roman.

"Oh, this is good," Franz Eddison said as Oliver stepped beside Roman in the hallway. "This is too good."

The picture Roman had found in Franz's prep room materialized in his mind so clearly that he could picture Liza tucked under Franz's arm.

He glanced farther down the hall, trying to see inside the open doorway at the end, looking for Liza.

"The whole city is after me, claiming I blew up the decontamination center, and I know it's something to do with you slummers."

The insult was directed at both Roman and Oliver, but Roman took offense for both of them. His body bristled as if he'd been struck with a hot iron. Roman was going to save Oliver's home, but first he was going to rip Franz apart. He removed the Byzing hand torch from his pocket and aimed it right between Franz's eyes.

"What are you doing here, Franz?" Oliver asked, far more civil than Roman could ever be.

"As if I'd tell you anything."

Roman squeezed the torch's trigger until the barrel glowed red. Not enough to blind or burn, but enough to raise the temperature in the hallway and make two beads of sweat run down the side of Franz's face.

"Hiding in your dad's office, if I had to guess," Oliver answered his own question. Franz didn't respond. "Listen to me, Franz. You don't have to like it, but Roman and I need to get into the power room. Icaria's falling and we're here to fix it."

Franz laughed, and Roman fought the urge to squeeze the trigger down all the way. He'd risk momentary blindness to silence that disgusting sound.

"Icaria isn't falling," Franz stated as a fact. "President Hinge stopped that when he locked *him* up." Franz didn't bother to look at Roman. "And when I hand you both over, my name will be cleared and I'll be rid of you for good, Oliver."

Roman stepped in front of Oliver, hoping his body would be enough to protect him from the oncoming flame of the Byzing torch. Before Roman could fully ignite it, the building shook. Roman's stomach evacuated into his throat and Franz lifted off the floor as the entire city dropped a foot. Tiny red lights flashed along the walls as some sensor shrieked a warning.

"This is really happening. The city is falling," Oliver said to Franz. He stood beside Roman and used the back of his hand to lower the torch until it aimed at the floor. "I know you've seen the readings. You work on this level too. You must have heard something."

"This is all his doing!" Franz shouted, pointing a finger at Roman. "Stealing our power and making us suffer!"

Franz ran forward. Roman rolled his eyes, but before he could stop the sunkisser and another one of his poor attempts at a punch, Oliver stuck out his arm and Franz ran into it, knocking himself to the ground.

Roman blinked, taking in the scene. In Bruno's warehouse, Roman thought it was Oliver's primal need for survival that spurred him into action. There was no need for Oliver to fight here when Roman was ready to do it for him.

"Bet that felt good," Roman half-joked to Oliver, but he ignored him.

"I'm sorry," Oliver said to Franz as he stepped over the sunkisser who sat on the floor, wheezing for air. The city seized again, and Roman and Oliver pitched forward as the entire building slid off-kilter.

Oliver may have been content with leaving Franz breathless on the ground, but Roman knew better. He bashed the handle of the Byzing torch against the back of Franz's skull, knocking him clean out.

"He'd call an enforcer," Roman explained as he followed Oliver to the power room.

Chapter Seventeen

Soft blue computer light soaked the hallway when Oliver pulled open the door to the power room. Digital screens flashed numbers and warnings. A worker sitting at the largest screen turned to face them, and at the sight of the two escaped criminals, she paled.

Her hand flickered to the radio on the desk behind her. Oliver tried to explain the situation; his voice devoured by the next shriek of warning bells just before the building rattled again. She brought the radio to her mouth, but her words were lost in the noise too. After another failed attempt of radioing an enforcer, the woman leapt toward Oliver.

Roman jumped between them and wrapped his arms around her throat, pinning her to his chest. The woman squirmed in his hold, her nails tearing into his forearms, but Roman didn't release her.

Once she fell unconscious, he dropped her body to the floor.

Oliver watched her chest rise and fall with shallow breaths. His horrified look shifted to something more akin to disgust. "Effective."

"Lock the door," Roman shouted over the computer's racket. Oliver would bash some slummer's head in with a metal rod without batting an eye but apparently drew the line at Roman knocking out a sunkisser.

He pulled off the backpack and wrestled out his sphere and tools. He tightened the horn that had rotated askew while in the bag and double-checked the measurement between the two points using the width of his fingers. When Roman felt certain his sphere was back to how he designed it, he tapped his Pada against the back and the small door popped open.

"What do you need?" Oliver asked, looking over Roman's shoulder at the sphere.

"Access to whatever point the grav energy comes to," Roman answered, yanking free a set of jumper cables from his bag.

Oliver led him to a steel-plated door in the back of the room. As they neared it, Roman's hair lifted off his scalp. He reached toward the dark iron rivets lining the door and a tiny spark bit into his finger. He glanced around the room but didn't see any of the protective suits he and Oliver wore out of the station back in the Slums.

"It's a hot room," Oliver explained while tapping keys on the number pad by the door. "Stay on the marked path or else you'll get the full taste of the energy."

"What'll I get on the path?" Roman lifted his fingers toward the steel door to feel the sting of the spark again.

"Just some tingling."

The door hissed as it swung open. The energy current slammed into Roman and knocked the breath out of his lungs. He had to wait for it to pass through him before he could step forward. The room was brilliant. It was terrifying. A lone coil stretched the full height of the expansive room. The thick metal rungs glowed with the blue gravity light. Bolts of energy zapped up the coil at random intervals.

"It should be like a heartbeat." Oliver stared at the coil. When a bolt reached the top of the coil, the building shook and the sensors from the other room screamed. "It shouldn't be so erratic."

The thing felt like Roman's heart: beating too fast. He took a deep breath through his nose and approached the coil. Even on the path painted in bright yellow stripes, Roman felt electrified. Part of him wanted to reach inside the sphere and see if his own hand could be the power source. Another part of him warned that it was a terrible idea. He couldn't be zapping away his limbs yet.

A railing wrapped around the coil as a poor attempt at protection. It was probably required by the head of some safety commission. It hummed with energy, and tiny bolts wiggled out of it and crashed to the floor. Roman clamped one end of the jumper cable to the railing. Blue energy festered around it and burned away the protective rubber coating before traveling toward the other end.

Roman inserted the other clamp inside the sphere just as the bolt reached the end of the cable. The tips of the horns on the sphere burst into blue light and a tiny ball of energy collected between them. Slowly, the ball spun in the opposite direction of the rings on the coil, siphoning away the excess energy. The shrieking outside slowed. The coil's heartbeat slowed. The static energy in the room became bearable.

"Ro, you did it!" Oliver said, admiring the coil as it returned to normal. When Roman didn't boast his own brilliance, Oliver looked at him. "Roman?"

Roman's fingertips buzzed. He felt each ridge of his finger pad pulse. The energy dragged across his fingers and spread into his hands and up his forearms. His Pada flashed rapidly before blacking out at the energy overload. His limbs became stiff and tight, and his heart beat uncomfortably in his chest, but he'd been in more painful situations. When he saw the energy arcs burning across the Slums, he'd figure the energy would do the same to him. He'd planned this part out, like he had everything else, but he hadn't realized that letting the blue light flow through him would feel this strangely. His hands locked around the sphere to ensure his grip. He wasn't able to make a long enough circuit within the sphere to start the reverse polarizing effect. Lucky for him, his long arms provided the extra length.

Once the polarizing effect was fully engaged, his sphere would operate without the extended circuit. He'd be too dead to see it in action, but seeing his sphere was never the plan. Roman wasn't dying to save this dumb floating city. He was giving up his throne in the Slums for

Oliver and Liza, for Scrap and Tansy. He only wished he could see the sun one more time.

Blue light shone under his pale skin. The gravitational energy flowed through his bloodstream. With the little control he had left, Roman forced his tired eyes to look at Oliver. The sunkisser was running straight for him. It was the last thing Roman saw before he blacked out like his Pada watch.

"Wake up, Ro," Oliver begged. "Come on, Ro. Wake up."

Roman's eyes burst open as a cold tear dropped on his face. He gasped and shot up, patting his chest and heaving in gulps of air. He looked around frantically. He didn't see his mom, or his grandmother. When his eyes latched onto Oliver's he understood.

"I'm alive?" he asked. "But the sphere . . ."

Roman looked between Oliver kneeling in front of him and his sphere hovering behind them. He grinned, the pain in his limbs forgotten as he watched his design work. The siphoned energy ionized within the sphere's horns before being sent back into the coil with new strength and improved stability.

"You're slanting brilliant," Oliver said to him, his expression mirroring Roman's, but his attention focused on Roman instead of the sphere. "Slanting reckless, though. You knew that would happen, didn't you?"

"I knew it needed some extra length to get started," Roman answered, and his grin didn't waiver. "I didn't know you'd shove me free of it. I didn't know it'd work after I let go."

"Well, lucky for you, it did."

"Me?" Roman laughed. "I was fine with dying."

"Whatever, Ro." Oliver pulled him off the floor. He kept his arm extended behind Roman, ready to catch him if he fell. "Is this thing stable now?"

"For now," Roman answered. "You'll want to make spheres for all the beams. I left blueprints in my backpack, but I guess I can help you now."

Oliver shook his head and muttered, "O and Ro, back at it again."

Before Roman could picture it, he and Oliver building robots to save their cities instead of destroying other bots, before he could understand how he felt about a future like that, the door scraped open.

"Step away from the coil!" A warning shot embedded in the floor a few inches from Roman's boot. "Do it now!"

Roman growled, vibrations rattling his chest as the sound waves clashed with the remaining gravitational energy in his bones. If the bullet had been aimed any higher, it could have hit the coil, or worse, his sphere. He didn't almost give up his life to save this city just for another sunkisser to ruin it. They really didn't have any respect for the nice stuff they had. No wonder almost all of it ended in the trash.

"Dad?" Oliver asked, as he turned to face their attacker. "Liza?"

Roman snapped his attention to the doorway. Liza wasn't holding the gun like his paranoid brain had led him to believe, and neither was Mr. Flint. An enforcer standing at President Hinge's side aimed the barrel at Roman's chest. More enforcers filled the room behind the president, their dark forms backlit by the digital screens of the control room.

"Step away from the coil," President Hinge ordered a second time.

Mr. Flint had called Roman a bad influence on his children when they were still in the Slums. Roman had overheard the conversation while trying to sneak Oliver out of the house so they could watch a fight at the Ring. Roman had never believed it until today. Not when he'd put Oliver in the crosshairs of sunkissing royalty.

"No," Oliver said to President Hinge. He stepped in front of the sphere. His golden curls lifted off his head from static.

"Oliver," Mr. Flint warned.

"No Dad," Oliver said. "We aren't moving."

Roman stepped beside his best friend, but instead of raising his fists to fight, he held up his hands in surrender. He wouldn't let Oliver be shot because of him. Every fiber in Roman's body fired at the unknown feeling. Roman didn't know how to give up. But he knew how to protect his people.

"We didn't damage it," Oliver said to President Hinge. "Roman fixed it."

"I'd never believe that coming from a slummer."

Mr. Flint bristled beside the president, clearly feeling the backlash of the insult meant for his son.

"Check the readings," Roman demanded. Despite his passive stance he was still willing to fight. "If you can't tell from the coil itself, then let your computers tell you. Icaria is leveling out."

"He's right," Mr. Flint said, watching the rhythmic pulse of energy. "The coil is stabilizing."

The blue energy rings lapped up the coil in a regulated pulse. The ball of energy rotating atop the sphere harmonized with it.

An enforcer behind President Hinge confirmed the readings on the screens. With a frown, the president ordered his enforcer to lower the gun. Liza ran out from between them.

"Liza, stop!" Roman's panicked shriek froze both her and Oliver. "We weren't decontaminated."

She frowned, horror painting over her beauty. She stood so close to him, just a few steps away, but she felt as far away now as when Roman first lost her and Oliver to Icaria.

"Because you blew up the elevation platform," President Hinge said, looking like he got the final punch in a street fight.

Roman fired right back. "To save your asses. You were going to let this place crash. Did anyone know what was happening? Were you going to warn anyone in the Slums?"

"Your robot was sucking away all my power supply. Your kind didn't deserve—"

"You know Roman's bot wasn't capable of doing that," Oliver said, cutting him off. "The thing couldn't contain that much power. I showed you the data, but you wouldn't listen."

"I should've known you were up to something when you failed to bring him in like you told me you would," President Hinge said to Oliver. "Who's to say you didn't mockup those numbers?"

"Ro saved Icaria," Oliver said flatly, and the strange fluttering feeling appeared in Roman's stomach again. He blamed it on the gravity energy still running through him. "He saved everybody."

Mr. Flint addressed the room. "My son's telling the truth, sir. I examined the data myself days ago but couldn't believe it. Our grav reports confirmed it, however. The stations are failing because of a power overload. Not from a drainage. I'm guessing whoever invented them didn't expect them to operate this long."

"They probably thought we'd all be back on the ground by now," Liza added.

Roman wanted to laugh but thought better of it. Even if the acid rain was gone and Earth could return to the way it was in his grandmother's stories, he doubted any of the sunkissers would give up their lives in the clouds for reality. People could pretend not to see a lot up here.

"Oliver and Roman should be released," Mr. Flint said to President Hinge. "I don't think press about why you locked up two young men who solved our energy crisis would look good for your reelection numbers."

President Hinge chewed the inside of his cheek. "Someone wash these boys clean. I can smell the Slums all the way over here."

The president turned his back on them and the coil, then disappeared behind the enforcers in the control room. Liza smiled at Oliver and Roman. If she could smell them, she didn't mind the stink.

"We'll meet you outside," she promised.

Roman believed her.

The receding acid fog made the sunrise more beautiful than Roman could have imagined. Wherever the sunlight passed through the fog, a dozen tiny rainbows exploded on the other side. Roman reached out to grab one, but the colors faded against his fingers. The bite of acid against his skin didn't burn as much as it had earlier that night. He turned his face to the sky and relished in the heat from the sun. It warmed him so softly, unlike when Oliver helped him escape Icaria. He opened one eye to look at the sun, but the brightness still burned, and he was forced to shut his eyes.

Oliver and Liza led the way down a quiet street. The building that housed the elevation platform was in ruins, but the mechanism that brought the carriages over the edge of Icaria remained operational. One waited for them on the platform. Its chrome exterior glimmered in the light.

"You know you can stay here," Liza said as they approached the carriage. "With us. With family."

Roman lowered his gaze, blinking to erase the red sunspots from his vision. "I have a family down there, too." He thought of Scrap and Tansy. Of Mr. O'Neal. People that looked out for him when he didn't always deserve it. After his parents died, after the Flints left, the Slums and its people took him in. He would always be a slummer.

And he was alright with that.

"Plus," Roman added before Liza could look too hurt at his comment, "I don't think Hinge would like it very much if I stayed. I did beat up that kid Franz a few times, and an enforcer."

"Not like that would stop you." Oliver grinned and pulled Roman into a hug. "I'll come visit. So will you."

"I'll think about it," Roman said after releasing Oliver.

Liza slammed into him next. Roman inhaled her daffodil scent. He'd come back just for that. Just for her and her brother. His sunkissing family. "You *will* visit."

"I'll visit," he promised.

Roman stared at it all again—the city, the sun, Oliver, Liza—and his eyes watered. He slipped inside the carriage before either of the Flints could see.

"I'll be down in a week for those blueprints!" Oliver shouted.

"O and Ro back at it again," Roman finally said it to him. "See you around, *filos*."

Chapter Eighteen

The Ring buzzed with excitement as the fight approached. Even in his prep room on the highest floor, Roman could practically feel the plexiglass windows shake from all the voices. Below him, both slummers and sunkissers filled the stands. It was getting harder to tell them apart. The slummers didn't look like skeletons when they stood next to the well-fed sunkissers.

Roman picked at his dinner sitting on a workbench. Every bit of the salad was grown in the Slums. The lettuce, cucumbers, and tomatoes harvested from rooftop gardens thriving under artificial grow lights. It was all thanks to Oliver. Whenever he wasn't building the gravity stabilizers, Oliver was bringing Icaria tech to the Slums. It was a perk of his new position as Technology Advancement and Disbursement Officer. Part of the deal they arranged with Hinge to keep quiet about his mishandling of the failing gravity stations. Together, Roman, Oliver, Scrap, and everyone else helped elevate the Slums without ever using an elevation platform. Real food, clean water, actual building supplies; Roman watched his city improve tenfold in just a year.

His prep room door slid open, and Oliver huffed his way in, running a hand over his hair.

Roman set down his fork and said, "You're cutting it close."

"I know, I know." Oliver smashed a few keys next to a computer screen taking up most of the side wall. "That air filter was not as simple as I thought it would be. Thing about snapped in half. I'll have to redo the rivets and—"

"Take a breath." Roman knocked his fist against Oliver's shoulder. "You can worry about that tomorrow. Tonight, there's only one thing to do."

The stillness before a fight always calmed Roman. The clarity just before he stepped into the arena was a high he'd chase his whole life. Roman turned away from Oliver and his coding screen to stare at their Rex bot. The beast loomed in the center of the room, ready to attack. Its chrome teeth glistened in the fluorescents. The cursive F and four-pointed crown were repainted in gold atop its snout. A bit of wiring hung between its claws. The innards from last week's competitor were all that remained from that fight.

"Do you ever get tired of winning?" Oliver asked with a chuckle.

Roman pulled the wire out of the bot's claws and grinned. "Never."

"Good." Oliver tapped his Pada against the bot's snout and nodded at the reading. The robot was fully charged and ready to go. "Because we won't hear the end of it from Liza if we lose when she finally watches us fight."

"I'll get your filter fixed tomorrow," Roman decided. Once the air was cleaner, Liza could visit without the fear of getting sick. Despite how easy it was to tease her in the bubble suit she wore to visit, Roman wanted the Slums to be clean for everyone.

An overhead announcer called out the ten-minute warning. Roman cracked his knuckles before grabbing the controller off a worktable. The two tiny bots that resembled him and Oliver stood at either side of the stand. He powered on the Rex bot and its tail swished. The machine growled and steam fell from its mouth.

"Scrap really talked you into that?" Oliver chuckled.

"Makes it look cooler." Roman's smile matched their robot's: all teeth. "He's using it for his next bot, too."

Roman directed the Rex bot to step toward their exit door, and he and Oliver followed it.

"I just bet a hundred on us to win tonight," Oliver said, powering down his Pada after submitting his bet.

"Isn't betting on yourself illegal?" Roman asked, raising an eyebrow.

"It's a good thing I'm not the pilot tonight," Oliver answered, sounding a lot like a slummer and not at all like the sunkisser he still dressed like. "Besides, we can use the extra scratch for upgrades."

"For Rex or . . .?"

"Whatever we want."

Roman exited their prep room. The Ring's light and the cheering of the crowd welcomed him home.

Acknowledgments

As always, a huge thank you to my agent, Nancy, and Kurt and Erica from Speaking Volumes for making this book a reality! Thank you to my early beta readers at the members of the Upside Fiction Writing Group for helping this story find its robot legs.

My endless gratitude goes to the Queen City Fiction Writers who met Roman first and cheered for him the loudest. Mark, Crystal, Bill, Jodi, Mike, Nick, Anna, Sam, Tobias—I hope you know how much you guys mean to me and how much better you've made me as a writer.

This book was inspired by the Bad Omen's album *THE DEATH OF PEACE OF MIND*. I always say music is my muse, but truly this book would not be here if it wasn't for that album. I used both the music and Roman's story as an escape, and sharing *Failing Gravity* feels like I've come out on the other side of that grief.

Thank you to my husband, Charlie, for always listening to me ramble and watching online robot battles for research. Thank you to my mom, Maja, for always believing in me. Who would have thought I'd write a book featuring "beef on toast?" I love you both more than you know.

About the Author

Jordan S. Keller is a Cincinnati based writer whose love for stories started at a young age when she preferred to write in a spiral-bound notebook rather than play outside at recess.

The thirst for stories grew in college where she majored in print and radio journalism, sharing the lives of the incredible people who live in Eastern Kentucky through the city radio station and multiple area newspapers. She possesses a bachelor's degree from Morehead State University for Convergent Media.

She sharpens her writing skills while recounting the heroics of her Dungeons and Dragons characters over dinner and co-running The Central Cincinnati Fiction Writers Group.

Jordan S. Keller lives with her husband, their bearded dragon, a goblin disguised as a cat, a puppy with airplane ears, and fourteen koi fish inherited when they bought the house.

Now Available!

JORDAN S. KELLER'S

ASHES OVER AVALON TRILOGY
Book One – Book Two – Book Three

**For more information
visit:** <u>SpeakingVolumes.us</u>

Now Available!

TONI GLICKMAN'S

BITCHES OF FIFTH AVENUE SERIES
Book One – Book Two – Book Three

**For more information
visit:** SpeakingVolumes.us

Now Available!

CYNTHIA AUSTIN'S

THE PENDENT SERIES
Books 1 – 4

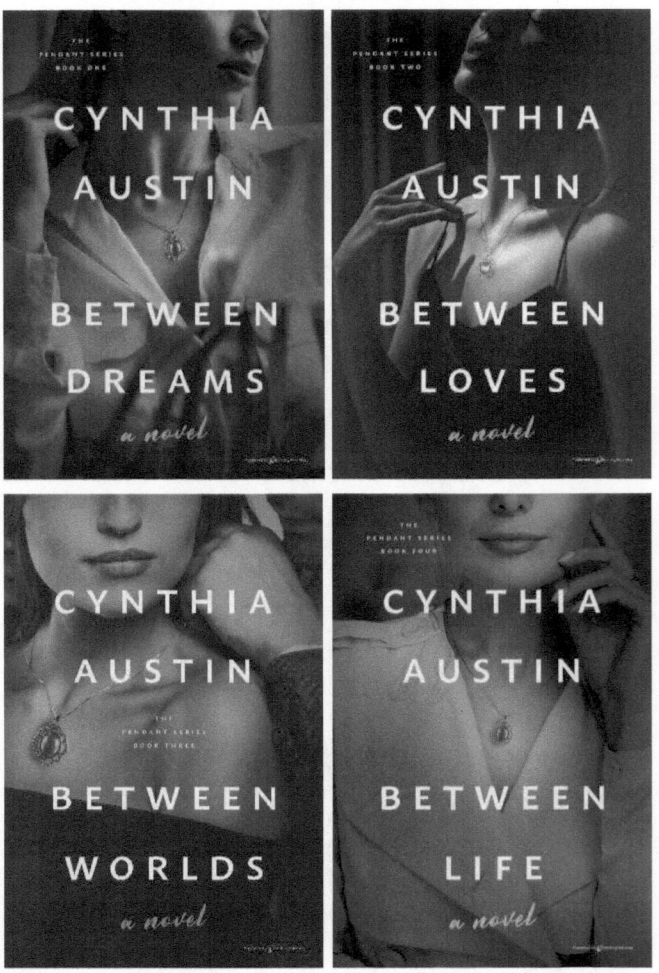

**For more information
visit: SpeakingVolumes.us**

www.ingramcontent.com/pod-product-compliance
Lightning Source LLC
LaVergne TN
LVHW041708070526
838199LV00045B/1254